MURDER AT THE COOKING SCHOOL

A Cedar Bay Cozy Mystery - Book 7

BY

DIANNE HARMAN

ISBN: 978-1516904853

CONTENTS

ACKNOWLEDGMENTS

Every time I get a favorable email or someone posts a compliment on my Facebook page, or tells me how much they enjoyed one of my books, I'm thankful and yes, amazed that I'm able to write books that people like to read. I thank you, my loyal readers, for making both the Cedar Bay and the Liz Lucas Cozy Mystery Series so successful. Murder in Cottage #6 was recently named as 'One of the Top 50 Self-Published Books of 2014 - 2015" by Readfreely, and I've been recognized as an Amazon All-Star author for many months because of the popularity of my books. It truly humbles me. None of this would have happened without you!

As always, a deserved shout-out to Vivek Rajan for his ability to turn my book cover requests into brilliant realities and for effortlessly formatting my books.

I'm so lucky to be married to my best friend who takes care of everything around the house, so I can follow my passion – writing. He's a harsh critic, but because of his attention to detail, he makes me look good. Thanks, Tom!

Lastly, in full disclosure, my husband I were fortunate enough to spend a week at a cooking school in Tuscany several years ago. All of the recipes in this book come from our time there. I've used them many times over the years, and I find them every bit as good now as they were when we learned to cook them in Tuscany. My biggest challenge while at the cooking school was figuring out how the chef made everything look so easy. Tuscany is a magical place, but fortunately we didn't have to deal with a murder.

Newsletter
If you would like to be notified of my latest releases please go to www.dianneharman.com and sign up for my newsletter.

DIANNE HARMAN

CHAPTER ONE

Kelly Reynolds, the owner of Kelly's Koffee Shop, one of the most popular places to eat along the Oregon coast, and her husband, Mike, the Beaver County, Oregon sheriff, were standing in front of the baggage carousel in the Florence, Italy, airport waiting for their luggage.

"Mike, I'm really, really tired, but I don't think I've ever been this excited in my whole life. I can't wait to see what the cooking school and the castle look like."

"I'm beat, too," Mike said. "That layover in Heathrow didn't help. I've never tried to sleep on a short hard surfaced couch in an airport with a gazillion people coming and going, and I want to tell you that it's not something I want to ever try and do again, but if that's what was required so we could get away from all we've been involved in recently, I guess I'll have to take it."

"Well, we'll probably have to go through Heathrow again on the way back, but for the next few days I'm not going to do anything but cook, drink some wine, and soak up the wonderful Italian ambience. I refuse to think about the murders we've had to solve. I'm so sorry your aunt was murdered, but I'd be a liar if I didn't tell you that I certainly appreciate you being the heir to her estate which made it possible for us to go on a very belated and long overdue honeymoon. Oh, I see our bags."

A few minutes later they walked through the airport doors and began looking for the white van from the cooking school, pulling their luggage behind them. The instructions the school had sent them indicated that the van would be picking up several people who were arriving around the same time to attend the cooking school. They were told to look for a white van with an Italian flag painted on the side.

"Mike, look over there. That must be it," Kelly said gesturing towards a white van with the flag of Italy prominently painted on the side. They walked over to it as a large man got out of the driver's side and took their luggage.

"*Benvenuti.* Welcome to Italy. My name is Alberto. I will be your driver during your stay at the *Castello di Nardo*. It will be a one hour drive, so please make yourselves comfortable. The other guests are already in the van. You're the last ones to arrive."

They stepped into the van and introduced themselves to the other six cooking school students. Within minutes they were on their way to a long overdue honeymoon and adventure. They never suspected that their romantic cooking school honeymoon in Tuscany would find them yet again in the midst of another murder investigation.

*****

Kelly and Mike spent the one hour drive to the castle looking out the window of the van at the beautiful Italian landscape while Alberto gave a running commentary about what they were seeing. He made several turns off of the *superstrada* or expressway and eventually turned onto a long driveway dramatically lined with enormous old cypress trees leading up to the impressive *Castello di Nardo*.

"A crude form of the castle was first built in the Middle Ages," the affable driver said, "and then during the Renaissance it was completely rebuilt and converted into an aristocratic residence called the *Castello di Nardo*. It has a private chapel which is situated in a panoramic position on a hilltop slightly above the castle. The property has belonged to the Nardo family for centuries. The state of art cooking school, which you'll be attending, is located in the castle which is situated in the center of the large estate where the family produces Chianti wine and olive oil which is sold throughout the world.

"The *Castello di Nardo* has recently been carefully renovated to make it into a boutique hotel. The architect and builder preserved the original rooms with antique furniture, large 17th century stone fireplaces, and floors made with terra cotta stone and marble. It's been equipped with every modern convenience such as central heating, Internet connection, satellite TV, and laundry service.

"The garden, which overlooks the valley below, is surrounded by very old trees, and on the large stone terrace there's an Olympic sized swimming pool with a Roman staircase lined with mosaics, two bathroom/dressing rooms, and plenty of lounging furniture. Next to the pool area is a hydromassage pool with access to a gymnasium and sauna. The entire terrace is lit up at night by large, wrought iron lamps. It's really quite spectacular," he said, passing through the entrance gate to the castle and coming to a stop in a large circular driveway.

The door of the castle opened immediately and an imposing, rather unattractive, woman walked out, accompanied by a younger man dressed in a traditional black and white hotel uniform. A huge dog stood on one side of the woman and on the other side was a dog that looked like a hunting dog.

"*Buonasera,* I am *Signora* Tonia Nardo. Welcome to my family's castle, the *Castello di Nardo*. I hope you enjoy your stay here. Matteo will show you to your rooms. Wine will served in the library at 7:00 p.m., and dinner will be at 8:00. If you need anything, please call the front desk."

The guests got out of the van and followed Matteo up the stairs while two young men unloaded the luggage and followed them. Kelly and Mike stared at the beautiful 18th and 19th century oil paintings which were casually displayed on the walls of the winding staircase.

Matteo showed the guests to their rooms, and as they entered the room where they would be staying while they were at the cooking school, Kelly and Mike both realized a great deal of money had been spent modernizing the castle. Electricity, running water, a flat screen television, and a telephone had all been installed. There was even a place on the desk for recharging cell phones and electronic tablets.

The antique furniture in their room looked like it had been in the castle for many years, if not centuries. Kelly had always enjoyed looking through magazines that featured antiques and stood in the middle of the room admiring the antiques surrounding her. What looked like a period lamp was on the nightstand, and a very old and authentic looking marble bust was prominently displayed on the dresser. If the furniture and furnishings hadn't been in the castle for centuries, someone had taken a great deal of care decorating it to make sure that both the castle and its rooms looked just as they had so many years ago.

"Oh, Mike, this is absolutely incredible. If the cooking school is half as good as what we've seen so far, this is going to be fabulous. Thank you again for coming up with the idea to spend our long delayed honeymoon at a cooking school in Tuscany. I think we're going to love this!"

"I couldn't agree more. We have two hours until we're having wine in the library. Think I'll try to grab a nap. Want to join me?"

"No. I want to look at this view. I don't want to waste a minute of our time here. Enjoy your nap, and I'll wake you in time for wine at 7:00 in the library."

The room overlooked a broad valley with rolling hills in the distance. Although it was just beginning to get dark, Kelly could easily make out the castle's vineyards and olive trees. She remembered being told by someone once that it was considered rude to ask how many acres of ranchland or farmland a person owned. Kelly assumed the same was true for vineyards, but she was sure that the Nardo acreage had to be in the many hundreds. It was stunningly beautiful. The paintings and photographs of Tuscany landscapes that she had seen and admired in books and magazines for years were reflected in the beautiful landscape before her as she stood nearly mesmerized, in front of the window admiring the view.

CHAPTER TWO

Luisa Bianchi, the chef at the *Castello di Nardo* cooking school said, "Sal, listen to me. I tell you I heard Tonia talking on the phone with that famous TV chef, Elena Oberti. Even someone like you must have heard of her. Since you don't do anything all day but lie around the house and watch television, I know you've seen her. She has her own cooking show on television. I'm sure Tonia's going to get rid of me, so she can hire Elena Oberti."

Luisa's husband, Salvadore Nardo, the brother of Tonia Nardo, the owner of *Castello di Nardo,* looked away from the television set and turned to her. "She can't get rid of you. She knows I'll tell her husband about the affair she's been having with Giovanni Rossi. No, that is just not possible. You must have misheard what she said on the phone."

"Listen to me, you stupid man. No wonder your parents gave her the castle. She is going to fire me, and then what will we do? The only other place I could teach cooking classes is at Berto Moretti's cooking school on the other side of the village, and he will never hire me. He hates Tonia and everyone who works for her, and if I don't work, we'll be out on the street. We have to do something."

"Luisa, I've been thinking," Salvadore said. "That castle should rightfully be mine. If it was mine you could teach even more cooking classes, and we'd get all the money that the cooking school brings in, not just some of it. I could run the hotel, and you could run the cooking school. I know my parents were always worried that Tonia's husband would get the castle if something happened to her, but remember I told you before we were married that my mother said they put a clause in their Wills that the castle would revert back to the Nardo family if anything ever happened to her. Guess what? Once my sister Tonia is gone, I'm the only member left of the Nardo family, and we'll get the castle."

"Of course I remember that. You've told me enough times."

"I know, but until now it wasn't all that important. Everything seemed to be going along fine. You worked at the castle teaching cooking, and I was able to stay in the house and take care of my medical condition."

"Sal, I would hardly call having a sore back from time to time a medical condition that keeps you from working. You have a degree in engineering, and you could find work without any problem."

"That's easy for you to say, but when you're an engineer oftentimes you're required to climb up into buildings and do other strenuous physical things. You know I can't do anything like that, because it might make my back worse than it already is."

"What you mean is that you wouldn't be able to drink grappa all day if you had a job. Sal, we need to do something. The only reason I agreed to marry you was that you told me someday we'd live in the *Castello di Nardo*." She looked around at the small dingy room of their tiny house. "This sure doesn't look like any castle to me."

"Yeah, well you told me you were going to be a famous chef, and to my knowledge, the only place you've ever cooked is in my family's castle, and that was only because I blackmailed my sister and got her to hire you."

Luisa sat down heavily at the foot of the couch where Sal was laying. She reached over and pushed the mute button on the television remote and said through the tears that were now streaming down her face, "Sal, we have to do something, now. Seriously, we'll be out on the street if your sister hires a new chef. If you're unwilling to do anything, maybe it's time for me to take action."

"What are you talking about? My sister wouldn't dare get rid of you. I don't think she loves her husband, but I sure don't think she'd want to be divorced either, and I don't see Giovanni Rizzo leaving his beautiful wife to marry my ugly sister. If she fires you, and if her husband finds out she's having an affair, he might leave her. So if both you and her husband are gone, she'd be all alone with no one to help run the cooking school. That's what I meant when I said she'd never fire you."

"I don't necessarily agree with you, but here's something I've been thinking about for some time. You need to get rid of your sister. If something happened to her, you'd be the sole and rightful heir to the castle, and our lives would forever change for the better. Things happen around castles. People take falls. Old buildings crumble for no reason and crush someone. When a woman or a man is out hunting, sometimes they're accidentally shot by another hunter, and often no one knows who shot them."

"Are you suggesting what I think you're suggesting?"

"Let's put it this way. If you don't take care of this situation within forty-eight hours, I will. Am I making myself clear?"

"Yeah, I get it. Now go get me some more grappa. I need to come up with a plan."

"Feel free to come up with one, because if you don't I'll put mine into effect. We belong in that castle, and I intend to be there very soon, one way or another."

CHAPTER THREE

It was a warm sunny afternoon on the outskirts of the little Italian village where Angelica Rizzo and her husband, Giovanni, lived amidst their groves of olive trees. She sat on the patio and enjoyed a chilled glass of white wine while she nibbled on some salami and bread which had been baked that morning by her cook. The setting was idyllic with the bright warm sun making the leaves on the olive trees even greener, if that was possible. She looked out at the spotlessly maintained olive groves where workers walked the rows daily to keep them free from weeds. If olive groves were ever in a contest for being perfectly cared for, the Rizzo groves would easily win.

Giovanni had told her he'd be late for dinner, because a client of his needed to see him about some legal problems he was having. Even though Giovanni had been a successful attorney for many years, he never used to let clients interfere with the time he considered sacred, the time he spent with his wife. She shook her head in frustration.

I know he's having an affair. Too many of my friends have hinted at it for it not to be true. I've tried to ignore the innuendos, but even though I'm dying inside, I'll never give anyone the satisfaction of thinking I know what they're talking about. I can just imagine what they must be saying. Probably that I'm stupid or blind. I'm sure I'm the laughingstock of the village, a pitiful version of the village idiot.

I didn't want to think the rumors were true, but after finding the receipt for the hotel in Florence, I couldn't ignore the situation any longer. I had to talk to someone, so I told my friend Luisa, the chef at Castello di Nardo. She patted my hand and told me Signora Nardo was gone from the castle on the same day as the date on the receipt. She'd told the staff that she had business in Florence. Right. She had business in Florence all right. Business with my husband.

She must be the reason Giovanni hasn't come to my bed for many months. I'm much prettier than she is, and people always tell me how warm and real I am. She's a cold domineering woman. I don't know what he sees in her. He never asks me anymore about what I did during the day or what I think about something. I'm glad I hired Piero to follow him and tell me if he's having an affair with Tonia Nardo. I wish Piero would call. I don't think I can go on like this much longer. I hired him a week ago, and surely he's found out something by now.

Angelica thought back to when she'd discovered the receipt in the bathroom wastebasket. She didn't make a habit of going through the trash, but the small bottle containing her contact lens solution had rolled off the bathroom counter and into the wastebasket. When she put her hand in the wastebasket to retrieve it, a bright yellow piece of paper caught her eye. It was a receipt for a room at the *Firenze Albergo*, the most expensive hotel in Florence. She stood looking at what some would call "firm evidence" for a long time, knowing her world was about to crash down on her. She couldn't ignore the situation any longer. With trembling fingers she picked up the phone and called her best friend Nuncia in Florence.

"Nuncia, it's Angelica. Do you have a minute? I need to talk to someone."

"Of course. What is it?"

She began to cry and for the first time Angelica completely unburdened herself. She told Nuncia about her suspicions, how her marriage had turned cold, how Giovanni seemed to have lost all interest in her, and her belief that he was having an affair with Tonia Nardo, the owner of the *Castello di Nardo*.

"Oh, *caro amica*, my dear friend, I am so sorry. I have met this

Tonia Nardo, and you are so much more of a woman than she is. What is Giovanni thinking? I have heard a term that Americans use when a man does what he is doing. It's called male menopause. I think that's what must be happening to Giovanni. Of course there will be no divorce. As strong Catholics, neither one of your families would ever allow it. First of all, before you confront him you must be certain. Several of my friends have used a private investigator they all highly recommend. I kept his name, because you just never know when you might need a good private investigator. His name is Piero. Here's his number. Call him, and tell him what you have told me. I'm sure he can help. Once you have the facts, you can decide how to proceed with the information. Again, *caro amica*, I am so sorry. I thought you and Giovanni had the perfect marriage."

"So did I, Nuncia, so did I. Thank you for the referral, and I'll call you after I find something out."

*****

Angelica's cell phone rang, and she saw Piero's name on the screen. "Piero, I've been waiting for your call. Have you found out anything?"

"*Si, Signora* Rizzo. I wish it was good news, but you asked me to find out what I could."

Angelica's heart was thumping wildly, and her knuckles had turned white where she was holding the stem of her wine glass. She took a deep breath and said, "Please, Piero. Tell me everything you found out."

"I cannot tell you my sources, but what you told me is true. Your husband and *Signora* Nardo have been seeing each other for many months. They meet at different hotels in Florence and Siena. Because I was not in their hotel room I can't say with certainty whether or not they are having physical relations, but then again what else do a man and woman do when they lock themselves in a hotel room for most of the day?

"I showed their photographs to a number of hotel personnel, and all of them recognized *Signora* Nardo and your husband as frequent visitors to their hotel. They stay in their hotel room from the time they get to the hotel until around 6:00 p.m. They arrive and leave in separate cars and usually order room service along with a bottle of wine. The room is reserved in his name, and he pays for it. I assume he pays with a business credit card, so the credit card bill would go to his law office, rather than to your home."

Angelica looked at her shaking hand and took a sip of wine. She clamped her hand on the stem of the wine glass and said in a high pitched voice that she barely recognized as her own, "Thank you Piero. What do your clients usually do after you give them news like this?"

"It depends. For some of them, the confirmation is enough. Others decide to take lovers of their own or confront their spouses. Rarely does the information I provide to a client lead to a divorce. Occasionally, people ask other things of me," he said and paused.

When he didn't continue, she said, "Piero, I don't know what you mean by other things. What else could there be?"

"*Signora*, the number I called is your cell phone, is that correct?"

"*Si*, but why would that matter?"

"I want to make sure that what I am about to tell you remains between us and is not traceable," he said. "Sometimes clients feel if the object of their spouse's attention is removed, the marriage can be saved."

The phone line remained silent for several moments while she digested what Piero had just said, and then Angelica replied. "Piero, I believe I know what you mean. I need to think about the information you've given me before I make a decision I might regret. I'll get back to you later today. If I should decide to do some other thing, as you put it, how much would you charge?"

"I have an account in the Cayman Islands. I would require that funds in an amount equal to twenty thousand American dollars be transferred to that account."

"Thank you. No matter what I decide to do, I'll call you later." She ended the call and poured herself another glass of wine, remembering the trust fund her parents had left her when they had died several years earlier. She'd never used it, because Giovanni made a very good living as a lawyer. They also had a nice source of income from the olive oil business which Giovanni had told her was thriving.

What better way to spend my inheritance than to once and for all get rid of the object of my husband's affection? I'd also probably be doing the community a service as well. I have heard talk that she is very cruel to her staff and has hurt a number of people, personally and financially.

She picked up the phone and pressed in Piero's telephone number.

"Piero, it's Angelica Rizzo…"

CHAPTER FOUR

Tonia Nardo put a tip in the young hotel valet's hand while he held the Alfa Romeo car door open for her. She waved to Giovanni who was in the car behind her and drove away from the *Firenza Aberigo*, easily entering the flow of traffic as she began the one hour drive back to the *Castello di Nardo*. In a few days a new cooking class would start, and she needed to make sure everything was ready.

She knew she was jeopardizing everything by continuing to meet Giovanni in hotels in Florence and Siena, but she couldn't help herself. Simply stated, she was madly in love with him. She lived for what he said and did to her during their private moments in the hotel rooms. For the first time in her life, a man made her feel wanted. She was very aware she wasn't the type of woman that men preferred. She was certain the only reason her husband, Stefano, had married her was because she had inherited the castle and its adjoining lands from her parents, who at the same time had cut her brother, Salvadore, out of their Wills. Stefano had even taken her surname, Nardo, as his.

Tonia was overly tall for a woman and very slender. Her figure, if you could call it that, was practically non-existent and was matched by her nearly flat chest. She painfully remembered being called "horseface" when she was in school. Tonia had never recovered from the acne she'd had as a teenager, and her face was permanently scarred. She lacked the grace and feminine characteristics that seemed

14

to be the birthright of other women, so her social graces were considered rough and coarse by those who knew her. Some said she was tone deaf, socially. Even with all of that, for the last year Giovanni Rizzo had declared his undying love for her, and she was eternally grateful for it.

It's so very complicated, she thought as she drove back to the castle. *He tells me how much he loves me, yet he is a very strong Catholic, as is his wife, Angelica. He tells me he wants to be with me all the time, but I know he'll never divorce her. I don't see how it will end. I suppose if I wasn't married, there's a chance he might leave Angelica, but I wonder. He's resolved all of the legal and financial problems I was having, and he tells me I'm through with those. He says if I deed the castle over to him, there would be no way that Stefano could ever get it. That would be true even if I died or divorced Stefano. Although legally it would be the property of Giovanni, he assures me it would only be for my protection, and he would never do anything without my consent.*

I've thought about his proposal for a long time, and I think that's what I'm going to do. With the cooking school and the hotel I've made enough money to pay the back taxes, and the government has taken their lien off of the property. I won't even have to do business with that shady man who said he would be willing to lend me the money if I would use the castle as collateral. He didn't tell me who he worked for, but I knew. It's common knowledge that the Mafia looks for people who are in financial trouble, offering to help them, and then they end up taking their property. No, if I deed the castle and its lands over to Giovanni, I will never have to do business with the Mafia.

Lost in reverie, Tonia almost ignored the ringing of her hands-free car phone. She looked at the monitor and saw that it was Stefano, her husband.

"Yes, Stefano, what is it?"

"I was getting concerned that you'd forgotten we have a dinner engagement tonight. We are due at the Bianchi's vineyard for a wine-tasting and dinner at eight o'clock. I'm just calling to remind you."

"Stefano, I haven't forgotten. I'll be there in just a few minutes, and I promise you we won't be late. You don't need to worry."

"I'm not worried about it, but I certainly don't want to do anything to upset our relationship with them. Their wine is some of the best in Italy, and it's always a favorite with the students who attend our cooking schools."

"I'm well aware of what our students like. That's the reason the cooking school has become so popular. Please make sure that Matteo feeds Bruno and Caesar. That's one less thing I'll have to do when I get home."

"Certainly. Where were you today?"

"Florence. I needed to add some extra things to the food I had ordered for the upcoming cooking school."

Stefano was quiet for a few moments, and then he said, "Couldn't you have just called and added it to your order rather than having to drive to Florence?"

"I probably could have, but I didn't. I'll see you in a few minutes."

She ended the call and thought how lucky she was that they had an arrangement. He had his friends, and she had Giovanni. She supposed it was his male ego that made him hint that maybe she'd had something else going on when she was in Florence. He would probably be very surprised that a man as handsome as Giovanni wanted to meet her in hotels in Florence and Sienna.

Even though ours is a marriage of convenience, I've always known about all your affairs, Stefano, but I never cared enough to confront you about them. Now you can see what it's like to wonder. Let's see, what was I thinking about before he called?

Oh, yes, I certainly hope Elena Oberti accepts my offer to be the chef at the cooking school. She's become very popular because of her television show, and I know she'd attract a lot of new students. Luisa is the problem. I don't think she'll accept a job as the sous chef under Elena, but I can offer it to her. If she does, it would keep my brother from telling Stefano about Giovanni, but maybe it's time to get out from under that threat. I don't think Stefano would care, I just think he'd be surprised that someone found me attractive enough to have an affair with. I don't see Stefano leaving me if my brother tells him about my affair with Giovanni. He likes to be the lord and master of the castle, and he certainly likes to oversee the vineyard and its production. It's a good thing it's not evident how much wine he's tested when we have the cooking school welcome dinners. Of course, anyone can tell from looking at his face that he has a fondness for the grape.

If I can get Elena to accept my offer, and she starts teaching at the castle, that should make my cooking school so popular Berto Moretti would have to close his, and I'd have the only cooking school in this part of Tuscany. If that happens, he would also probably have to close down that pitiful little shop of his, Cucina, and leave the area. When he leaves I will become the Queen of the Tuscany Cooking Schools. I think I'd like that title. What I'd really like to do is have Giovanni become my King, but since that probably isn't going to happen, I'll still continue to see him. If he wasn't in my life, I don't think I'd want to live. Stefano never has and never will mean anything to me, and I don't have anyone else. The children I so desperately wanted never came.

The only one who really loves me besides Giovanni is Caesar, my dog. Some might call that kind of pathetic, but I love it that I don't have to depend on anyone else for my happiness. No, I definitely have a good life, and even though I don't rely on Giovanni, he makes my life worth living. The next time we meet, I'll tell him I've decided to sign the papers deeding the castle over to him, so he can make sure that Stefano never gets it. I trust Giovanni with my life, and I know he has my best interests at heart.

She turned off the main highway and onto the road that led to the castle, refreshed and pleasantly satisfied from her day with Giovanni.

CHAPTER FIVE

Giovanni pulled out from under the hotel portico and then allowed Tonia to get ahead of him. Even though they were both going back to the village, he wanted nothing more to do with her. Several hours with her were as much as he could bear.

He looked in the rear view mirror to see how much traffic was behind him and was greeted with his own image. Giovanni had to smile, acknowledging to himself he still had the good looks that had opened doors for him throughout his life. His jet black hair was beginning to gray at the temples, accentuating his piercing deep blue eyes. His muscular body and mahogany complexion had always made him irresistible to the opposite sex. It was also what made him irresistible to Tonia.

I don't know how much longer I can keep this charade up, he thought. *The woman absolutely nauseates me, and the act I put on when I make love to her and tell her how much I love her would qualify me for what the Americans call an Academy Award. She's ugly as sin, and there's nothing warm about her. If she doesn't deed the castle over to me in the next few weeks, I'm going to forget about the whole thing. It's not worth the price I'm having to pay.*

He remembered when he first came up with the idea to seduce Tonia in order to get the deed to the castle. He was at a dinner party one evening and happened to be seated next to her. It was about the time he was becoming more and more desperate. He knew he had to do something to get money. He'd embezzled funds from a client for the first time in his career and knew with certainty it wouldn't be the last.

It was a typical spring evening in Tuscany, warm and inviting. Softly glowing candles were on each table and twinkling lights hung from the patio cover, making the evening magical. The wine flowed, and the scent of freesia flowers filled the air. It reminded him of his first kiss so many years ago. It was a night made for romance. Even though he'd known Tonia most of his life, he'd never before sensed how lonely she was for a man's attention, and that evening he'd given her plenty of attention. The candlelight, the wine, and the intoxicating freesia scent made her seem almost pretty. She'd recently converted the castle into a hotel with a cooking school, and she mentioned how profitable it was becoming. She told him she kept the financial books for the castle, and although she owed back taxes on it, soon she'd have enough money to pay the taxes and it would no longer be a problem. While she was talking, a plan began to form in Giovanni's mind.

She was like a puppy who wanted to be held and petted. Seducing her a few weeks later had been the easiest thing he'd ever done in his life and provided a way out of the hole he'd dug himself into. After they'd met a few times and become lovers, he casually approached her with his scheme. He'd told her how he wanted to make sure she was taken care of and how he worried about her. He said they both knew they probably could never be together as a couple because they were both married and strong Catholics, as were their spouses. He'd suggested she deed the castle over to him, but had done it in an offhand manner, as if it was a joke. In the weeks and months that followed, the joke had become a serious topic of discussion between them.

At first she had been adamant she would never do anything like that. She told him there was no reason for her to do it, but the more he wore her down with his talk of love and how deeply he cared for her, her resistance began to crumble. He knew he was very close to getting her to do it.

He thought about why he was doing it. The funds he'd embezzled from clients over the past year had gone to pay for a lot of things his wife, Angelica, took for granted. She thought he made a lot of money, but if the truth were known, every month was a struggle to try and pay the bills. He knew that Angelica had a large trust fund, but even as amoral as he'd become, taking his wife's money to pay for his mistress' apartment was something he couldn't stoop to do.

Giovanni had rented the apartment last year for Maria. Just the thought of Maria caused warmth to spread through certain parts of his body. He hadn't meant to fall in love with someone twenty years younger, but when her father had come to his office one afternoon for a consultation and brought his beautiful blond daughter with the bedroom eyes with him, Giovanni knew he had to see her again. No woman he had been with had ever come close to awakening the passion he felt when he was with Maria.

There is nothing I wouldn't do for her. I have to get the castle, so if anyone ever finds out about the embezzlements, and if the legal examiners disbar me, I could sell the castle and take care of her. Maria and I both know I won't marry her. I can't, but I have promised her that I want her to be my mistress for the rest of my life, and in order to keep my promise, I need the castle.

If Tonia deeds the castle over to me, she'll no longer be of use to me. I know I've broken the oath I took when I became a lawyer by embezzling money from a client, and I've certainly broken marital and moral laws by having so many affairs. Even so, I've never been responsible for causing someone's death, but it's the only answer to my problems. I don't think I have a choice anymore. I know that when I get the castle and sell it, Tonia will claim I got it from her illegally or some such thing, which will create all kinds of problems and might even cause me to lose the castle to her. If she's not around, it will be much easier.

So Tonia, enjoy each day, because the day you deed the castle over to me will be one of your last days.

CHAPTER SIX

"Mike, wake up," Kelly said as she gently shook his shoulder. "It's time to go down to the library and sample what I'm sure will be some delicious local wines. I'm going to shower. I'll be finished in just a few minutes, and then the shower is all yours. There's a really good mirror here in the room I can use while you're showering."

"Kelly, I feel so much better. Thanks for letting me take a quick nap. What did you do while I was lights out?"

"Sat in the chair and looked out the window. I can't get over the beauty of Tuscany. It's like a magical land and these accommodations, they're spectacular. I've never stayed in a castle. Matter of fact I've never been outside the United States. Anyway, I watched while someone lit small decorative lanterns in the vineyards and the olive groves. It's an absolutely beautiful nighttime scene."

Showered and refreshed, they made their way downstairs. Following the sound of voices, they entered the library where wine was being served by *Signora* Nardo and a man they assumed was her husband, *Signor* Nardo. He was as round and genial as his wife was ramrod thin and rigid looking.

What a strange couple, Kelly thought. *Signor Nardo must be six inches shorter than she is and outweigh her by a hundred pounds. From the broken capillaries on his cheeks and nose, it looks like he thoroughly enjoys drinking the wines he produces in his vineyard.*

Signor Nardo walked over to them, introduced himself, and shook their hands while an ear-to-ear smile lit up his florid face. He had a large, droopy mustache and a mane of unruly prematurely white hair.

"Please," he said, "let me get you some wine. We're very proud of the wines we grow and serve in the area. Would you prefer red or white? Personally, I think they're all good, but I've learned people usually have a preference."

The red and white wines of the Tuscany region were known throughout the world by wine connoisseurs. Kelly and Mike couldn't believe the array on the sideboard in front of them. Reds that bore the names of Vino Nobile di Montepulciano, Brunello di Mantalcano, and Chianti Classico along with whites such as Cortona Sauvignon Blanc and Vernaccia di San Gimignano were all being freely poured. It was a wine connoisseur's paradise, but unfortunately neither Kelly nor Mike was a wine connoisseur.

"I prefer a red," Kelly said. "What do you recommend?"

"You must try the Brunello. I'm told it's one of the best. Try a sip and tell me what you think."

Kelly swirled the wine in her glass and tried to look like she knew what she was doing. After a moment she took a small sip. "Whoever told you that is absolutely right. It's wonderful. I'd like to try some of the others, but I think I've already found my favorite. Thank you."

Signor Nardo turned to Mike. "What can I get for you?"

"I'd like to try a white, whatever you think is good, although if you have them here, I imagine they're all good."

"I like all of them, but why don't you try the Vernaccia? Friends of mine make it, and it's one of my favorites."

Mike took a sip. "That's simply wonderful. Thank you."

"Bring your glasses and I'll introduce you to the other guests who will be in your cooking class." Introductions were made, wine loosened tongues, and after some small talk, the group of ten made their way into the dining room.

Dinner was just as fabulous as the wine that had preceded it. Kelly and Mike loved Italian food, but they both knew chefs often felt they couldn't leave well enough alone, adding their own touches and losing the essence of the dish. Not so at *Castello di Nardo*. The entreé was a simple loin of pork that had been slow cooked in milk with fresh vegetables and prepared in the classic Italian tradition. It was peasant food at its best, enhanced by freshly baked parmesan and olive oil bread that was called *pane con olio e parmigiana*, and a salad that tasted as if it had been brought in directly from the garden. The meal ended with a selection of fresh fruit.

Mike was seated next to *Signora* Nardo. "I don't think I've ever tasted food that was this fresh. What's your secret?"

"What we don't grow on our own property, we get at local farmers' markets. Luisa, the cooking school chef, will take you into Florence to the *Mercato Centrale* in the heart of Florence. It's open every day, and it has the best of everything. There are a number of others in small towns around here we go to when we don't have time to go to Florence.

"We have chickens here and also raise most of our own meat. I think you'll enjoy breakfast tomorrow morning. The fresh eggs, local bacon, and fruit are usually a hit with our guests. Our resident cook comes in early to bake muffins and some other breakfast items. It's too dark now, but in the morning you will be able to see the orchards, our large vegetable gardens, and at this time of year, probably some pheasants. If you enjoy eating, you'll not do any better in Italy than here at *Castello di Nardo*. If you'll excuse me, I need to introduce Chef Luisa so she can tell you about the cooking school."

Signora Nardo stood up and lightly touched her water glass with her knife several times to get everyone's attention. When they were quiet she said, "It is my pleasure to introduce Chef Luisa Bianchi to you. She has been teaching here at the *Castello di Nardo* since we opened the cooking school. Her background in cooking is impeccable. She had a restaurant in Florence for many years that was given three stars by Michelin and then decided she'd prefer to teach cooking. She travels throughout Italy teaching at cooking schools in various places. We feel very fortunate that she comes to *Castello di Nardo* four times a year to teach. We have many more applicants than we have space for, so consider yourselves very lucky to have been accepted. Here is your teacher for the next week, *Capucuoco* Luisa Bianchi."

The students applauded as a short, round grey-haired woman who looked exactly like what one would think an Italian grandmother, a *nonna,* would look like, entered the room and smiled broadly. When she smiled, her round face squinched up making it hard to see her eyes. She wore a white apron with the words "Castello di Nardo" embroidered in red on it. She brushed a stray hair back into her severe bun with fingers whose nails were short and free of nail polish and began to speak.

"Welcome, my new students. In Italian the word for chef is *capucuoco,* but I prefer to use the word chef. It is so much easier to pronounce. My English is good, but not perfect, so if I make a mistake, please forgive me. For the next three days a continental breakfast and coffee will be served in the dining room each morning from seven to nine. Class will start at ten. At that time we will begin cooking for lunch and dinner. We will eat lunch on the patio at 12:00. After that you will be free until 4:00 in the afternoon. From 4:00 to 6:00 we will prepare the rest of the evening meal. Wine will be served in the library at 6:30 followed by dinner in the dining room. I have two assistants to help me, but I do request that each of you volunteer to be a server for at least one meal. You will be given recipes for everything we prepare.

"The highlight of the day trips will be Wednesday when we will go to Florence to the *Mercato Centrale.* It is one of the most incredible markets in the world, and it is usually a high point for the students. On Tuesday we will go to an olive grove and see how olive oil is processed. If you prefer, you may stay here at the castle and swim in the pool or simply relax. It is your time to do what you want, and there will be no pressure to participate in these afternoon side trips. The only thing I do ask, as I said earlier, is that each of you helps serve one meal. I think that's everything. You will be given a kitchen apron tomorrow morning with your name on it. I would ask that you not wear rings while you're preparing food as we often use our hands in the preparation of the food. I will make sure all of your hands are very clean by having one of my assistants watch while you wash your hands," she said laughing. "See you at ten tomorrow morning."

When she was finished, Mike stood up and said to *Signora* Nardo, "Thank you for an enjoyable evening. This has been a wonderful beginning for our stay in Italy." He turned to Kelly and said, "We need to get some sleep before the big day." They walked around the table and said good night to the other guests and to *Signor* Nardo.

When they were back in their room with the door closed, Kelly turned to Mike and said, "Did you get a chance to find out what the other people do for a living, like own fancy restaurants or what ?"

"Oh, Kelly, this is one of the things I love about you. You're worried that someone will be a better cook than you, aren't you? That's adorable. Trust me; you will be the best student in the class. I'll go with you to class tomorrow, but after that I may explore the countryside or walk the grounds or do nothing but lie in bed and read a book. You know I'm not much of a cook, and I have no intention of becoming one. I'm just happy to be in Italy with you in this remarkably beautiful place."

With a slight sound of trepidation in her voice, Kelly said, "I hope you're right. I have to admit I'm a little nervous. What if someone asks me what I do, and I tell them I own a coffee shop, and then I can't cook as well as anyone. I've never done anything like this."

"Trust me, sweetheart, you'll be fine. I love you," he said, lightly kissing her and turning off the light on the nightstand. "Sleep well, and we'll try to keep jet lag at bay."

CHAPTER SEVEN

"Mike, you've got to see this," Kelly said the next morning as she looked out the window. "This view is incredible, and you can see forever. Oh, my gosh! There's a whole covey of quail in the vineyard. There's a bunch of little ones walking behind their mother. It's one of the cutest things I've ever seen."

He walked over to the window and joined her. "Honey, I agree. This view is absolutely beautiful. It looks like something you'd see in a travel magazine or on one of the travel television shows. Just think, for the next few days we have no cares and nothing to do but eat good food, look at a beautiful landscape, and drink some great Italian wine. I am so ready for this vacation, but before I do anything else, I need coffee."

"Give me five minutes, and I'll be ready. I'm curious what the cook's prepared for breakfast. I can always use some new ideas for the coffee shop."

"I think you'll be going home with a notebook full of ideas and recipes. I've never tasted pork as tender as the one we had at dinner last night. Have you ever cooked pork in milk? I don't remember seeing you do that."

"No, I've read about it, but I've never done it. It doesn't seem to be all that difficult. I wonder if that's one of the recipes we'll get."

"I have no idea. That's your department. Crime is my department," he said flippantly.

"Well, glad your department is closed for a week. You need some time off, and I think we've found the perfect place for it."

When they got to the bottom of the stairs they heard the sound of strained voices and sensed the tension in the air. Mike raised an eyebrow and shrugged his shoulders in answer to Kelly's unasked question. Two policemen stepped out of a nearby room and approached them. One motioned for Kelly to follow him, and the other one asked Mike to follow him. They took them to separate rooms.

"What is going on?" Mike asked. "What's happened?"

"We're not sure, but there is a strong possibility that *Signora* Nardo has been murdered," the policeman said. He asked Mike where he had been for the last several hours and then said, "Please don't take this personally. We have to question everyone who was in the house last night."

"I understand. I'm a local county sheriff back in the United States, and I would do the same. Can you tell me more about what happened to *Signora* Nardo? I'd like to talk to your chief and offer my help."

"He would probably like to have help from someone who is staying here. You might be able to learn things we can't. All we know is that her maid discovered her body when she went into her bedroom this morning at 6:00 a.m. She told us that every morning she takes *Signora* Nardo a tray with a cappuccino and two cornets or croissants filled with jam. She said it never varies."

"Was anyone with the maid?" Mike asked.

"No, she was by herself when she went into the *Signora's* bedroom. The maid said it was very strange because the *Signora* looked like she was asleep, and in all the years she had been employed by *Signora* Nardo, she was always awake when the maid entered her room. She walked over to *Signora* Nardo's bed and noticed that her skin was almost blue, and she wasn't breathing. She picked up the phone and dialed security. Immediately one of the castle guards came in the room and said that the *Signora* was dead. He called us. That's all we know. Follow me, and I'll take you to the chief."

A few minutes later as Mike walked down the hall to the room where the police chief was interviewing people, he saw Kelly in the dining room. "Excuse me," he said to the policeman, "I need to tell my wife that everything's all right. I'll be back in a minute." He walked over to where Kelly was standing. "Are you okay, sweetheart?"

"Yes, but I can't believe she died last night right here in the castle. The policeman asked me a few questions and realized I didn't know anything. Do you think the police suspect foul play and perhaps she was murdered?"

"I don't know, but I'm going to offer my services to the chief of police. I know I'm on vacation, but I'm sure I'm the only law enforcement person who's actually staying here at the castle. Also, the fact that I speak English like most of the other guests might be of some help. Maybe I can find something out."

"I was thinking the same thing. We've had good luck solving crimes before. I'll do what I can to help you."

"No, emphatically not. You are not to help in any way, shape, or form. You are here to enjoy our honeymoon and pamper yourself for one week while we're here in Italy. You are here at the castle to cook, not to solve a crime. I'll take care of that. Am I making myself clear? I want your sincere promise you won't get involved in this."

"If you insist," she said, mentally crossing her fingers behind her back and wondering who she should talk to first.

"Good. I'm glad we have an understanding. I'm going to talk to the chief. I have no idea how long I'll be gone. Get something to eat, and I'll meet you in the kitchen when the cooking class starts a little later. When I told you I probably wasn't going to be doing all that much cooking, I certainly didn't think I'd be spending my spare time helping the local police."

"I would think the chief would be thrilled to have your help. Go on, I'll see you later. Here's a cup of coffee to take with you."

"Thanks. You're always looking out for me, and I love it!"

CHAPTER EIGHT

"You must be Mike Reynolds. My deputy told me you're a sheriff in the United States. I'm Police Chief Carlo Varano. The castle is in my district. I understand you would be willing to help me if the *Signora's* death turns into a murder investigation," he said, extending his hand to Mike. "And until I hear otherwise from the coroner, I've decided to treat *Signora* Nardo's death as a murder. That way I can start my investigation now, rather than later."

"Yes, I'd be happy to help in any way I can. It would be presumptuous of me to say that I could help solve the case, but feel free to let me help you in whatever way you need. I thought since I'll be staying here in the castle for a few more days I might be able to be your eyes and ears," Mike said. "By the way, I'm surprised you speak perfect English."

"I'm fluent in English. I was born in Italy, but my mother, who was a widow, sent me to live with my uncle in the United States when I was a young boy. I lived there for nearly twenty years then returned to Italy when my mother became ill. You may notice I even have a little bit of a Brooklyn accent."

The chief continued, "I can use all the help I can get. The Nardo family is quite well known throughout Italy, and I anticipate there will be a great deal of media coverage regarding *Signora* Nardo's death, particularly if it turns out she was murdered. Let me tell you what I know. *Signora* Nardo's death occurred sometime late last night or early this morning. The coroner has already been here and will be doing an autopsy this afternoon. That's how important the Nardo name is. If she didn't die from natural causes, his initial feeling is that she was poisoned, since there were no signs of injury to her body. Naturally we will be developing a list of suspects."

"It's been my policy to always start with who has the most to gain when someone is murdered. Did she have children? What about her husband?" Mike asked.

"The Nardos did not have any children, and from what her staff has told me, she always felt it was a great tragedy that she couldn't bear children. They said she had contacted many specialists throughout the world, but she never could get pregnant. Her husband is supposedly devoted to her, although that's what they usually say."

"Do you know if she had a Will?"

"*Signor* Nardo says both of them had Wills which named the other as the sole beneficiary of their assets. Actually, his real name is not Nardo. He took her family name after they married. The castle has been in her family for centuries, and the Nardo name was far better known than his family name of Drago. With her death the castle and the surrounding properly all becomes his."

"I know it's very early in the investigation, and what I'm going to say is extremely simplistic, but it sounds like he would have a very good reason to murder her. I imagine this castle and the land is worth a great deal of money."

"Yes, it definitely is. That would be in addition to the thriving olive oil business and the wine that is produced here, both of which are sold world-wide at a substantial profit," the chief said.

"Again, I know it's early in the investigation, but have there been any instances of marital discord? Have there been rumors of either of them having affairs?"

"You're right, it is very early in the investigation, but from what the staff has told us, even though the Nardos seemed as different as night and day, he was certainly devoted to her, and there were no outwards signs of marital discord."

"The policeman who talked to me mentioned that *Signora* Nardo was discovered by her maid. Where was *Signor* Nardo?"

"In Italy it is very common for people who have been married a long time to have separate bedrooms, if they can afford to do so, and obviously the Nardos could afford to do so. He was in his bedroom having breakfast. From what her maid told me, she takes *Signor* Nardo his breakfast and the morning papers and then takes *Signora* Nardo's to her. *Signor* Nardo did not find out about the murder until he was told by the castle security guard."

"How is he taking her death?" Mike asked.

"As expected. He's in shock and can't believe it. I briefly talked to him, and if it turns out she was murdered, he can't imagine who might have killed her or who would have any reason to want her dead."

"That might be true, but I've seen too many wives and husbands over the years put on a very good act when it comes to the death of a spouse. I'm not saying he did it, it's just always the first place I look when a spouse has been murdered."

"In that we are alike. I will be investigating both of their private lives as well as those of the staff here at the castle, but as of right now, there are no suspects. Here's my card. I've written my cell phone number on the back. Please call me if you hear or see anything I should know about."

"Something just occurred to me. When we arrived yesterday afternoon, *Signora* Nardo had two dogs with her. I haven't seen them this morning. Would they have slept in the room with her?"

"I wondered about that as well. Every time I have come to the castle her dogs have always been with her. One of them is quite a protector. People in Italy buy the courser breed for just that purpose. They don't attack unless they are told to by their owner. Many wealthy Italians own them as guard dogs. The other dog is her hunting dog. The *Signora* was known to be an excellent shot and loved to hunt. Her maid told me that after she retired, one of the staff members always took the dogs to the dog run. The dogs were brought to her room when she had finished breakfast."

"So if she was murdered, the dogs would not have been in her room. Seems kind of odd she would own a dog for protection, and yet it wasn't with her at night. Where are they now?"

"They're in the dog run behind the castle. Even though they are both perfectly trained, *Signora* Nardo knew that Caesar, her courser, terrified a lot of people. To be honest, he terrified me the first time I saw him. He weighs about one hundred fifty pounds and it's all muscle. When she entertained she often put them in the dog run to put her guests at ease. There is a dog house for each of them in the run. Bruno is her Italian pointer and has a very sweet disposition. I don't think he's ever intimidated anyone. Her maid told me that *Signora* Nardo thought only peasants slept with dogs in their room, and she refused to do what the peasants do. If she was murdered, being a peasant during the nighttime might have saved her life."

"I have a guard dog," Mike said, "and he sleeps with us. Maybe I'm a peasant. Each to his own. I'm sure you've considered that her death might have been a suicide."

"Yes, of course we're looking into that possibility, but so far we've found nothing to support it. We'll know more after we get the coroner's report. Usually when a person commits suicide, they want to punish someone, or there is a history of mental instability. There was no note or anything else to indicate that suicide was the cause of death, and I've never heard anything about *Signora* Nardo being mentally unstable."

"Here's my cell phone number," Mike said. "If you want me to look into something specifically, feel free to call me. I'm sure things will begin to surface soon."

"I appreciate your willingness to help. Enjoy the cooking school. I've heard very good things about it."

"Thank you, and I'll talk to you soon."

CHAPTER NINE

As she made her way down the stairs, Kelly heard voices coming from the hallway that led to the kitchen where the cooking classes were being held. She knew she was quite early for the class, but she was nervous and thought getting there a little early would help overcome her nervousness. She hesitated, not wanting to intrude on the conversation. She clearly heard two women speaking in Italian. What surprised her was that she understood almost all of what they were saying.

When she'd been in school she'd taken several Italian classes, but she hadn't spoken it for years and had been certain none of it would come back to her. A few weeks before they left for Italy, she'd gone to The Book Nook, the book store her friend Ginger owned, and purchased a couple of books on Italian, hoping to refresh her memory. She thought it would be fun to be able to say a few phrases and maybe understand a word or two. What really surprised her was that it all came back to her. She felt like she was picking up something she'd learned yesterday instead of many years ago.

Kelly had gone back to the The Book Nook a second time and bought a novel written in Italian, curious if she'd be able to read it. It was as if she was back in school. She read the book from front to back and never questioned a word. She knew the real test would come when she was in Italy and actually heard people speaking Italian. She also knew that seeing something in print and hearing it could be two very different things. She wanted to surprise Mike, so she hadn't mentioned it to him.

She stood very still, her curiosity overcoming the rudeness of her eavesdropping. The women were talking about *Signora* Nardo. "The police don't know it, but we all do. There were a lot of people who would have liked to see her dead," one of them said.

"Well, I'm not going to be the one to tell them, are you?" the second woman asked.

"No. I don't want to get involved, plus if one of them killed her, I could be the next one."

"It could have been her brother. They've fought for years over this property. From what I've heard he always felt he should have inherited it, not her. He's a good-for-nothing, so I'm not surprised her parents gave it to her. Don't forget about Berto Moretti. My friend tells me he'd give anything if his cooking school was as popular as hers. He has to discount what he charges to get anyone to even attend, because it's everyone's second choice. They all want to come to the *Castello di Nardo*."

"What about Giovanni Rizzo. The *Signora* didn't think anyone knew about her relationship with him, but everyone did. She told people he was her lawyer, which he was, but that wasn't all he was. Do you think the *Signor* knew about them?"

"I don't know, but I heard that *Signora* Rizzo knew. And I know something I don't think anyone else knows. *Signora* Nardo met with a man who promised to loan her a lot of money if she would use the castle as collateral. Rosario in the village was here the day he came, and she said he was Mafia from Sicily. *Signora* Nardo did all the bookkeeping for the two of them, so I don't think her husband knew they were very badly in debt before she converted the castle into a hotel and started the cooking school."

"I don't know what to think. As cruel as she could be to the people who worked for her, many of the staff members would be more than happy to see her dead. There's no way she would commit suicide. She thought she was above everyone. She never would have done that. Her health was good, so I'm convinced she must have been murdered. What else could it be?"

"Well, I wasn't the one who killed her. I don't like being around dead people, and believe me, I've seen enough to know I don't want anything to do with the police. Let's not speak of this again. I have to go to the kitchen to help Chef Bianchi, and I don't want to be late. She can be a very demanding chef."

"Tell me about it. I'm glad I'm not working in the kitchen with her. I had to do it the last time she taught a cooking school here, and it wasn't one of my favorite things to do. I'll stick with cleaning the guests' rooms. Like you, I won't be talking about this to anyone."

Kelly could tell from their fading voices that the two women were no longer in the hallway. Her heart was beating wildly, and she wondered if she should go back to the room and tell Mike what she'd overheard. The two women had unwittingly provided a lot of information she knew would take Mike and the police chief a long time to find out.

I'll tell him later. He's probably still with the police chief, and I really don't want to be late to the first cooking class, particularly after listening to those two women talk about Chef Bianchi. I wonder what we've gotten into here at the Castello di Nardo.

CHAPTER TEN

Kelly walked into the kitchen where the cooking classes were going to be held and looked around in surprise. She thought she'd be the only one nervous about the cooking classes, but the fact that everyone was there early made her think she wasn't the only one who was anxious about them. One of the chef's assistants walked over to Kelly and handed her an apron and a notebook with the recipes they would be making that day with Kelly's name written on the front of it. Kelly looked at her and assumed she was one of the women Kelly had heard talking a few minutes earlier. She looked around for Mike, but he wasn't there. Even though she was fifteen minutes early, she was the last one to arrive.

The class consisted of ten people. She recognized them from dinner last night. There was the couple from Michigan who thought it would be fun to do something together, because they normally took separate vacations. They were already at the castle when the rest of the students had arrived yesterday. At dinner Kelly had learned she liked to shop and he liked to fish. This cooking class vacation was a compromise for both of them. There were four women from Alaska, all of whom were accomplished cooks, at least to hear them talk. The last two members of the group were two men who owned a restaurant in Omaha, Nebraska. They wanted to expand the menu in their restaurant so that it included some authentic Italian dishes, as that type of food was becoming very popular in Omaha. She'd talked to all of them last night, and with the exception of the couple from Michigan, all were passionate about their love for food. She was looking forward to getting to know them better.

"Since everyone is here but Mike Reynolds, I think we'll begin," Chef Bianchi said. "Pasta waits for no man, and I would have to say the same about the preparation of food. Anyway, the chief of police told me Mr. Reynolds may be late and probably wouldn't be attending many of the classes since he was going to be helping the chief. Probably all of you have heard that *Signora* Nardo died sometime last night or early this morning. As of now the police don't know what the cause of death was, but I want to assure you that the cooking school will continue as planned. I know *Signora* Nardo would want us to do that. Please pick a partner and form into groups of two. You will work with different people each day, but I've found it makes it easier to have the same pairings for lunch and dinner. Kelly, since your husband isn't here, I will be your partner."

Swell. I could have done without that. The chef and I are going to be partners. In my worst case scenario, I never considered that this might happen.

"Thank you, Chef. I'll look forward to learning from you," Kelly said.

"I will go to each of your stations," Chef Bianchi said, "and tell you which dish or dishes I want you to prepare and how far you can go in the preparation of it. The stations have been set up with what you'll need for your dish. Naturally, finishing touches will be done by the servers and my assistants as needed. The purpose of this school is to familiarize you with Italian cooking. Unlike the French, we are not precise. A dash of this, a little of that, changing out one ingredient for another if it's in the same family of ingredients. It's really very simple.

"All that's needed for a wonderful Italian meal is an entrée, a salad, a vegetable, and a dessert. Traditionally, the Italian meal consisted of five courses which always began with a pasta course, but recently that has changed, and pasta courses are often considered to be the entrée. We will be preparing all of them. You are welcome to ask me any questions you might have. I will be teaching you how to make things from scratch, such as pasta and bread. I realize many of you work outside of the home and wouldn't have time to make these on a daily basis, so that's why conveniences such as packaged pasta, sauces, and other things are readily available. Shortcuts are sometimes necessary, but I caution you to use only the best of ingredients and shortcuts. Don't waste your time and money on cheap things. The food you serve always reflects the integrity of the ingredients. For example, never cook with a cheap wine. If a wine is good enough to be served at dinner, it should also be the one you use in a recipe. Never settle for second best."

She turned to Kelly and lowered her voice. "Kelly, we will be making a classic risotto entrée, which is a dish that Italy is well known for. It is a very difficult dish to make properly, but I have mastered it, and I will show you how, but first I must tell the students what to do. Read the recipe directions and begin to prepare it. I'll be back to help in a few minutes."

Swell, just swell. A classic risotto. I've never made a risotto in my life. Why couldn't it be something with Nutella? I've pretty much mastered anything with Nutella. I mean what's not to like about chocolate and hazelnut? I will never forgive Mike for not being here. I might not even tell him about the conversation I overheard. That would serve him right for making me have to partner with Chef Bianchi.

She leafed through her book of recipes and found the one for the mushroom risotto. She read it through and started by putting the dried mushrooms in warm water. Then, according to the directions, she peeled and finely diced an onion. She was assembling the ingredients for the stock when Chef Bianchi returned.

"Good. I see you're soaking the mushrooms, and you've peeled and diced the onion. You can go ahead and make the stock. It has to boil for an hour, and then it needs to be refrigerated. We will serve the risotto at dinner this evening. I would like you to be a server tonight, so you can follow the recipe from beginning to end. I noticed on your application that you own a coffee shop. This might be a dish you could serve there. Please continue. I have to see how the other students are doing."

Kelly followed the directions and brought the broth to a boil. When an hour had gone by, she very carefully took a sieve and removed the vegetables. Once again, she brought it to a boil and cooked it until it was reduced by half. Chef Bianchi returned several times and finally said, "That looks good. As I mentioned earlier, it has to be refrigerated until we're ready to use it in the final preparation of the risotto. Lunch will be served shortly. Why don't you join your husband on the porch? I saw him talking to the wine steward a few minutes ago. I wonder if he's found anything out about *Signora* Nardo's death."

"I have no idea, but Mike is very good at solving crimes. Did you know the *Signora* well?"

"I have known her and her husband for many years, but I can't say she was a friend of mine. She was not a woman who had many friends. Although I travel throughout Italy, I consider the little village down the road my home, and I live there when I'm not teaching. One hears many things in a small village like mine, and there has been a lot of talk about the *Signora* and Giovanni Rizzo. His wife is a good friend of mine. We went to school together and have remained friends ever since. She has suspected for some time that the *Signora* and Giovanni were lovers, but I don't know. I shouldn't be telling you this, but you're very easy to talk to, and ever since I heard about her death this morning, I wondered if *Signor* Nardo had found out about the affair and killed her."

"Thank you, but I can't believe it was *Signor* Nardo. He seems like such a nice man, even though they did seem very different from each other." Kelly said. "By the way, I really enjoyed this morning's session. I am embarrassed to tell you this, but I have never made risotto. It's one of those dishes I've always heard is very hard to cook properly."

"It is, but as I said earlier, I've mastered it. You'll put the finishing touches on it before dinner tonight and from now on, you'll be able to easily make it."

"I hope so, because I love to eat it. Last night you mentioned that in addition to the excursion to the *Mercato*, we would have the opportunity to visit an olive oil factory and grove. I've never seen how olive oil is made, and I would be very interested in seeing it."

"Alberto will be driving us there tomorrow afternoon following lunch. Actually, you'll have a chance to meet my friend Angelica Rizzo then. She and her husband, the lawyer, are the ones who own the olive grove we will be visiting."

"I remember last night hearing that there is an olive grove on this estate that produces olive oil which is sold throughout the world. I'm surprised we're going elsewhere."

"The Nardo grove is quite small in comparison to the Rizzo grove. The one on the Rizzo's land is one of the largest in the world. It's only a few kilometers from here to their estate. I'm sure you'll enjoy it. Excuse me, but I need to make sure that everyone is getting close to finishing what needed to be done for lunch and dinner. See you later."

Well, she actually seems pretty nice, Kelly thought as she walked out to the porch. *I know the two women I overheard spoke disparagingly about her, but so far she's been very gracious to me. I didn't hear her tell anyone they were stupid or that something had been done totally wrong. Of course she may have a public persona and a private persona. I'm glad she suggested I join Mike on the porch. It will give me time to tell him what I overheard.*

"Well, hello, big guy," Kelly said to the large dog that was sitting on the porch. "You must be Caesar." At the sound of his name the big dog wagged his tail and nuzzled Kelly's leg.

"Oh, sweet boy, I'm sorry about your owner. If you're lonesome, I'd be happy to be your friend. I miss my dogs, Rebel and Lady, and we could adopt each other while I'm here."

She turned away from the big dog and walked over to where Mike was talking to a man she presumed was the wine steward the chef had mentioned. She looked down and saw that Caesar had decided to follow her and was walking right next to her.

I guess he took my offer literally. He probably misses his owner. I can't take her place but maybe we can be friends while I'm here. She reached down and petted him. He looked up at her with big brown eyes as if to say,

"Thank you and yes, let's be friends."

CHAPTER ELEVEN

Kelly was walking over to where Mike and Domenico, the wine steward, were standing when one of the staff motioned to the wine steward. He excused himself and followed the young man into the wine cellar.

"Well, I see it didn't take you long to find a new friend," Mike said, kneeling down and petting Caesar.

"I think he's lonesome, and we're kind of bonding. Anyway, I miss Rebel and Lady, so I don't mind having him around. I imagine he won't be welcome in the kitchen, so you might have to watch him when I'm attending class."

"What I'm wondering is who's in charge of him now. I understand from the chief that *Signor* Nardo is in mourning and refuses to see anyone or take any calls. The chief told him he wanted to see him tomorrow, but he'd respect his need for privacy today."

"Mike, I overheard two women who work here talking about the *Signora's* death. They didn't know I could hear what they were saying. I think you and the chief might be very interested in what they had to say."

"I imagine they were speaking Italian, and I suppose you just happen to know Italian, and you've never told me about it. Right?"

"Actually you're right, but it will have to wait until after lunch," she said as he looked at her with a raised eyebrow, clearly doubtful. At that moment the students from the cooking class walked out onto the porch and everyone began taking seats at the long table that had been set up on the porch. The view was incredible. It was a warm sunny day with a bright blue sky overhead and rolling hills below. Kelly felt as if she had entered a Tuscany painting.

The long narrow table easily accommodated the ten cooking class attendees. It had been set with white linens, silverware, crystal glasses, and flowers in small vases. Three glasses were at each place setting. There was a stemmed glass with a round bowl for red wine, a stemmed glass with a cylindrical bowl for white wine, and a regular glass for water. When everyone was seated the wine steward stood at the head of the table and began to speak.

"I know you were welcomed last night by *Signor* and *Signora* Nardo, but as the wine steward for the cooking classes, let me welcome you as well. My name is Domenico. At the top of your place settings there are three glasses. At each lunch and dinner I will be pouring premier wines from the local area, both red and white. The wines will be different at each meal. I will put the bottles on the table, and after I pour your wine, feel free to help yourselves to more. If you like the wine, you may wish to write down the name on the label so you can purchase it after your stay at *Castello di Nardo*. You are welcome to try both of the wines or just one. If you prefer not to have wine with your meal, please turn your glass upside down. Enjoy," he said as he began to pour white wine into the glasses, soon followed by the red wine. Three large water pitchers had also been placed on the table.

Mike turned to Kelly and said, "This is delicious. Did you make any of it?"

"No. I made the beginnings of risotto which I'll finish preparing just before tonight's dinner."

After the students had passed the generous antipasto platter and the focaccia bread around the table they were served a plate of salad consisting of lettuce, pears, parmesan cheese shavings, pine nuts, and hazelnuts.

"Mike, the dressing on this salad is delicious. I never would have thought of this combination."

The woman to the left of Kelly said, "I'm glad you like it. I made it, and it was really easy. Just a little olive oil, lemon juice, and pepper. But wait until you see what's for dessert. The students at the station next to me were making it, and it was all I could do not to sneak a bite when they weren't looking, but I thought that might be kind of tacky," the woman who was from Alaska said smiling.

"You can't leave us hanging. What is it?" Mike asked.

"It's one of the most interesting desserts I've ever seen. Kind of a walnut cake with a strawberry sauce. It looked beautiful, and I can't wait to try it."

A few minutes later after the servers removed the luncheon plates, they returned with plates of the thinly sliced cake topped with strawberry sauce. Kelly took a bite and turned to the woman, "Your instincts were absolutely right on this one. It's delicious. Did it look difficult to make?"

"No, not at all. This is one I definitely want to try when I get home."

"I can already see it on the Kelly's Koffee Shop menu. Would I be right, Kelly?" Mike asked.

"You know me too well. Yes, this is definitely going be on the menu. When I get back to our room I want to circle it, so I don't forget it. If we're going to have food like this at every meal, I think I better take up jogging or something like that while we're here."

"Well, funny you should mention that because the wine steward told me bicycles are available if we want to ride into the village or just take a ride. That might be fun. Matter of fact you might want to take a bike ride this afternoon, because the chief is picking me up and taking me to the station. He called right before you came out and told me the coroner finished the autopsy this morning, and he has the report. He wants to talk to me about it."

"Actually, I need to talk to you before your meeting with him. I think you'll both be interested in what I learned earlier, and yes, I do think I'll take a bike ride to the village. I'd like to take Caesar with me, but I don't know who I should ask to get permission for him to go with me."

Caesar had worked his way between Kelly and Mike's chairs, and it was becoming apparent that Kelly had found a friend who was definitely going to be with her the rest of her stay.

"First of all, I can't wait for you to tell me how you just happened to overhear a conversation in Italian and understand it. That should be a good story, and remember, I don't believe in coincidences. As far as Caesar, I don't think I'd worry about it. If he acts like he wants to go with you, I'd let him. Maybe you should ask one of the staff if he has a leash, or maybe there's one in the dog run." He looked at his watch. "The chief is picking me up in forty-five minutes. Let's go back to the room. It looks like everyone else is beginning to leave as well."

"Mike, I'd like to make a quick stop at the dog run. I want to see if I can find a leash, although since Caesar weighs more than I do, I'm not sure what good it would do me, but it might make someone else feel a little safer if they see that the huge dog is on a leash."

A few minutes later they returned to their room with a heavy black leash. Caesar had walked up the stairs with them and followed them down the hall. Although they'd passed several staff members, no one seemed the least bit concerned that Caesar was with them.

CHAPTER TWELVE

When they got to their room, Mike shut the door and turned to Kelly. "All right, I'm ready to hear your story."

Kelly sat down on the edge of the bed and began, "We've never talked about whether or not either of us spoke a foreign language. When I was in school I took a number of classes in Italian and seemed to have an ear for the language. Actually, I'm pretty good with a couple of languages. They come very easily to me. I remember when I had cooks working for me at the coffee shop who were Mexican, and after a couple of weeks I could understand almost everything they said."

She told him about the books she'd gotten at The Book Nook and how she was going to surprise him. When she saw the skeptical look on Mike's face, she walked across the room to where the maid had set out an Italian newspaper for them when she'd cleaned their room. Kelly picked it up and began translating the lead article that had to do with the President of the United States, and how he and his family were coming to Italy to meet with the Pope.

"Okay, Kelly, you've made your point. I believe you. Now tell me what you overheard."

She spent the next twenty minutes telling him what the two women had said and concluded by saying, "I don't know if you want to tell the chief about it, but it might be something he should know."

"Let me get this straight. You've been in Italy less than twenty-four hours, and you just happened to overhear a conversation which indicated that if *Signora* Nardo was murdered there are five possible suspects. Remember, I won't know until I learn from the chief and the autopsy report if she was murdered. But let's say she was, and let's say what you heard was correct."

Kelly interrupted him, "Mike, what I heard was correct. That's what I overheard."

"Okay, I'll play along. *Signora* had a good-for-nothing brother who was jealous of her because she inherited the castle and the land. Then there's her lover's wife. Uh-huh. Oh, I don't want to leave out the Mafia man. I mean anytime there's a murder in Italy a member of the Mafia has to be involved." He deliberately avoided her gaze which was getting steelier by the moment.

He continued, "I don't want overlook the owner of the competing cooking school and last, but not least, her husband, *Signor* Nardo. Kelly, doesn't this all seem a bit too convenient? Maybe those two women wanted you to overhear them. Maybe one of them killed *Signora* Nardo and was trying to draw attention away from herself."

"First of all, they didn't know I was there, and secondly, even if they had known, why would they assume I spoke Italian? No one knows about that except Ginger, the owner of The Book Nook. She remembered when we were in school how much I'd loved Italian. Certainly no one here knows."

He was quiet for a few moments. "Okay, I'll grant you that. It just seems too coincidental that you, of all people, would overhear that particular conversation. You're probably the only one here besides me who has been involved in solving crimes."

"That's probably true, but Mike, sometimes things can't be explained logically. It just is what it is. I think this is an 'isness' time, at least that's the word I use when something just is and can't be rationally explained."

"An 'isness' time? Would you like me to tell the chief that you heard this conversation because it was an 'isness' time? That would go a long way to establishing my credibility with him."

"Quite frankly, I don't care what you tell him, if anything. That's your decision. I'm just telling you what I heard," she said jumping off the edge of the bed and flouncing into the bathroom.

When she walked out a few minutes later, Mike said, "I apologize. I was being a smart aleck, and that wasn't fair. You're absolutely right about sometimes things happen for no apparent reason, and this is probably one of those times. I'll see what the chief has to say about the autopsy report and then decide whether or not I should tell him what you overheard."

"That's fair. Anyway, I just heard the conversation. I never saw who was talking. It could have been idle gossip or there could be some truth to it. What makes me think there is some truth to it is that Chef Bianchi said pretty much the same thing about *Signora* Nardo and Giovanni Rizzo. Evidently his wife is one of the chef's best friends, and she's been worried for a long time that they were having an affair."

"Why would she tell you that?"

"She said I was easy to talk to. She was wondering if you'd found out anything, and one thing led to another. I think she regretted mentioning it after she said it."

"I would imagine she did. I've got to leave. See you later," he said, lightly kissing her and patting Caesar on his head as he walked to the door.

"I'll probably be in the kitchen when you get back," Kelly said. "The chef asked me to be a server tonight, so I could finish the risotto. I'm going to be leaving now, too. I don't have much time until I have to report back to the kitchen. I'll be curious what the report has to say."

"You're not the only one," he said as he walked out the door.

CHAPTER THIRTEEN

Kelly and Caesar went down the stairs to the front desk of the castle. "Matteo," she said to the young man who had escorted them to their room the day before, "I was told you have bicycles available for the guests. Would it be possible for me to ride one into the village?"

"Of course. Follow me. I see you have made friends with Caesar. He was *Signora* Nardo's dog. Caesar usually doesn't mingle with the guests. I was surprised to see him come down the stairs with you."

"He probably senses that I love dogs. I'd like to take him to the village with me. Do you think that would be a problem?"

"No, it will be fine. Actually, it would probably be a good thing. While we have very little crime around here, oh, maybe a petty theft or two, we prefer it if the guests don't leave the premises by themselves, but if Caesar is with you there won't be a problem," he said as he opened the door of a storage shed and took out a bright blue bicycle.

"He doesn't seem like he's particularly aggressive," Kelly said.

"I've never known him to be aggressive. I would say he's protective. You don't need to worry about having him in the village with you. Is there some place special you're going?"

"I own a coffee shop back in the United States, so I love to go to shops that have cooking things for sale. I assume there's one in the village."

"Yes. It is called *Cucina*. It's not a very original name. It means kitchen in Italian. Go to the second stop sign when you get to the village and turn right. It's down about half a block on the right hand side. You can't miss it. There's a large blue awning with the word "*Cucina*" written in big white letters on it. *Signora* Nardo didn't want the staff to tell any of the guests about it, because it's owned by Berto Moretti. He's the man who owns the other cooking school in our area. There is bad blood between the Morettis and the Nardos. They don't speak to each other. Our cooking school has always been much more popular than his, but it's not surprising because Chef Bianchi is considered to be one of the best chefs in Italy. *Signor* Moretti is very tight with his money and won't pay to have a top-notch chef come to his cooking school. He opened the shop in the village hoping to get tourists to stop in and then sign up for his cooking school. When our school is sold out, he winds up getting the students who can't get in here."

"Thanks Matteo. If I don't leave now, I'll never be back in time to finish my risotto for dinner tonight. I don't want to make Chef Bianchi angry."

"No, that you don't want to do. She doesn't get angry often, but when she does, you definitely don't want to be around her. She and the *Signora* did not get along. I really don't know why. On the surface the *Signora* was always nice to her, but one time I heard her tell *Signor* Nardo that she hated Chef Bianchi because she acted like she was so important. I remember him asking her why she'd hired her, but I didn't hear her answer."

"That's interesting. I never would have thought that. She was very gracious to Chef Bianchi at dinner last night."

"That was part of a show for the guests. When the guests weren't around, it was pretty clear they really didn't like each other."

"Thanks again, Matteo. I'll see you later. Where should I put the bike when I return?"

"Just leave it out in front, and I'll put it back for you."

*****

There were signs leading to the small village when she got to the end of the lane that led to the castle, and Kelly was there in a very short time. Even if there hadn't been signs, Caesar knew the way. She easily found the shop called *Cucina*, got off of the bike, and tied Caesar up to a pole in front of the shop. She knew that was probably unnecessary, but it made her feel better.

She was prepared to not like the shop based on what she'd heard about the owner, but when she opened the door she was pleasantly surprised. She hadn't realized the shop also sold some food items which filled it with wonderful aromas. One wall featured balsamic vinegars from every region in Italy. On another wall bookcases were stuffed with Italian cookbooks. All kinds of kitchen utensils were displayed on the shelves in the small shop, many of which she'd never seen before. It was colorful and charming.

"Welcome to *Cucina, signora*. How may I help you?" a bearded dark-haired young man asked.

"I just want to look around if you don't mind. This is a wonderful shop. It must be a joy to work here. I've never seen so many different kinds of balsamic vinegar."

"I'm not surprised. My father loves balsamic vinegar."

"Oh, you're the owner's son?" Kelly asked. "I understand he also owns a cooking school just outside of the village."

"That's true, and it's considered to be the best in the region. There is another one near here called *Castello di Nardo*, but many of the people who come to our school have already been to that one, and they tell us they much prefer the warm atmosphere at ours. *Signora*

Nardo, God rest her soul, was not the warmest person in the world."

"I don't understand why there happens to be two cooking schools so close together in a remote area like this. Which one was here first?"

"My father's was the first one. *Signora* Nardo opened hers later. There is talk she ran out of money, and in order to maintain the castle she had to make it into a boutique hotel and a cooking school. She has a brother who doesn't work. It is well known in the area she hired his wife to be her chef for the classes. Their parents willed the castle and the land to her. From what I hear," the young man said conspiratorially, "when he found out she was going to have a cooking school in the castle, he threatened to tell her husband about the affair she's been having with Giovanni Rizzo if she didn't hire his wife to be the chef. *Signora* Nardo had no choice. I heard that the *Signor* wondered why she had hired her sister-in-law, but she convinced him she was a very good chef, and she would be much cheaper than anyone else they could hire."

"That surprises me. I thought the chef at the school had owned a very famous restaurant and traveled all over Italy giving classes."

The young man laughed. "None of that is true. You must be staying at the castle and taking her classes. That's the story they tell people and who checks things like that out when they're going to a cooking school? No one. It has presented problems for us because my father refuses to do that. No, believe me, the only other kitchen Chef Bianchi has ever been in is her own."

"Do you have any cookbooks from your cooking school? I own a coffee shop in the United States, and I'm always looking for new things to serve."

"Of course. Actually there are several. We don't have just one chef. We have some new ones and some returning ones and many of them have their own cookbooks. All of the cookbooks on that middle shelf are from cooks who have taught at our school," he said, gesturing towards the shelf. "The problem is that they're all in Italian.

I don't have any in English."

"That's not a problem. I speak Italian. Thank you. You've been very helpful. I can only stay a few more minutes, but I would like a couple of the books. Let me take a quick look and see which ones I want."

Ten minutes later Kelly walked out of the shop and put the three cookbooks she'd purchased in the bike basket. She untied Caesar from the pole and said, "Okay, Caesar, it's time to go back to the castle. I wonder who's in charge of feeding you tonight. I better find out. I don't want you to starve." The big dog loped alongside the bike as they made their way back to the castle in the deepening late afternoon shadows.

CHAPTER FOURTEEN

When she got back to the castle, Kelly left the bike near the front door, and she and Caesar walked in the front door. "Oh, Matteo, I'm so glad you're here. Where can I find some dog food for Caesar?"

"It's in the little shed that's in the dog run. He gets fed there," he said, looking at his watch. "Actually, it's about time for the dogs to be fed. *Signora* Nardo always fed them around 4:30, because she didn't want them to be hungry when dinner was served to the guests. I'll do it right now."

"Thank you. I think Caesar is a little hungry after our trip to the village. I'm running late, and it's my turn to serve tonight, plus I have to finish up the risotto. I'll go up to my room and get my apron. Thanks again for helping me with the bicycle."

A few minutes later she walked into the kitchen where the other servers and assistants were gathered to put the finishing touches on the evening meal. Just as the evening before, wine was being served in the library, although the Nardos were not pouring tonight. The wine steward had taken over that task for the duration of the cooking class.

"Kelly, there you are. You need to finish up the risotto. I want you to start by bringing the stock you made earlier to a simmer. Melt the butter and add the onions. Cook them over a low heat until they're almost translucent and then add the mushrooms. I'll be back in a minute."

Kelly did what Chef Bianchi had told her to do. When the chef hadn't returned after a few minutes, Kelly looked at the directions, removed the mushrooms and added the Arborio rice to the mixture. She continued adding the broth as needed.

Chef Bianchi has a lot more confidence in my ability to properly cook this risotto than I do. I wonder where she is and when she'll be back. I can't leave the risotto. Guess I'm stuck with preparing it, and I hope I'm doing it right."

A few minutes later Chef Bianchi returned. "Sorry, I had to make a telephone call. You've done a very good job, Kelly. Please continue while I check on the other students," she said walking around to the different preparation and cooking stations. Kelly noticed something moving just beyond the kitchen door and saw Caesar lie down and stare at her from across the kitchen.

I think we've bonded. Wish I could take him home, but don't think that will work. I kind of remember reading you have to quarantine household pets that are transported to the United States from a foreign country, and anyway, I'm not so sure Lady and Rebel would like the competition, particularly Rebel.

"All right students," Chef Bianchi said a half hour later. "You're excused. My assistants and I will finish up here. Please feel free to go into the library and enjoy a glass of wine. I'd like the two servers back here at ten minutes until eight."

Kelly took off her apron and draped it over the stool in front of her station. She walked into the library with the others and saw Mike talking to the wine steward. "Kelly, how did your risotto turn out?" Mike asked.

"Actually it was a lot easier than I thought it would be. You can tell me how I did after you have some for dinner. I think you're going to be very happy with the dinner from what I saw in the kitchen. I'd like a glass of the white wine," she said to Domenico, the wine steward. He poured her a glass of white wine and then turned to take the requests of the other guests.

Mike put his hand on her elbow. "Why don't you come out on the porch with me? The sun is setting on the hills and the entire countryside for as far as you can see is bathed in a soft golden light. It's really quite beautiful."

They walked out the glass doors which were encased in Mediterranean pine. "Mike this is gorgeous. The colors in the sky are going to the soft mauves and blues of early evening. What a spectacular sight. I'm so glad you thought to bring me out here to see it."

"Yes, it's beautiful, but that's not the real reason I wanted to come out here. I found out from the chief of police today that *Signora* Nardo was murdered. The coroner's report indicated she was evidently given a large dose of sleeping pills and then given a lethal injection of a substance which evidently caused her to die instantly. The coroner said it might take weeks to find out exactly what the substance was, but whatever it was, it resulted in her death."

"Oh, no! Mike, that's terrible. Now what?"

"Well, I felt kind of silly telling the chief of police what you'd overheard today, but he was very grateful as it provided him with a place to start. He said he intends to investigate each one of the people you heard the two women talking about, and he's asked me to help him."

"Mike, I biked into town today with Caesar and found out something interesting." She told him about her conversation with Berto Moretti's son.

"I'm not surprised," Mike said. "The chief told me that although the Nardo family is very well known in this area and has been for centuries, *Signora* Nardo was not very well-liked. He finds it hard to believe that Giovanni Rizzo would have had anything to do with her. Carlo said Giovanni's wife, Angelica Rizzo, is a beautiful woman and loved by everyone and her husband, Giovanni, is a very handsome man. He told me it was common knowledge that Giovanni had had many affairs, but they'd always been with a beautiful woman, and *Signora* Nardo was definitely not beautiful."

"You know, Mike, there's an afternoon excursion tomorrow to the Rizzo's olive oil processing plant located on their estate. I'm going to take that trip. Maybe I'll have a chance to meet Angelica Rizzo and find out some information about her relationship with not only her husband, but also with *Signora* Nardo."

"You're on your own for that. The chief is picking me up tomorrow morning, and I'll be spending the better part of the day at the police station with him. He's very interested in finding out if *Signor* Nardo has an alibi for last night when *Signora* Nardo was murdered, and likewise if the *Signora's* brother, Salvadore, has an alibi. I did find out something interesting that I don't think you know."

"What? And by the way, I think there's a whole lot I don't know."

"*Signora* Nardo's brother, Salvadore, is married to Chef Bianchi."

"Well, I heard the same thing from *Signor* Moretti's son. Do you know why she uses the name Bianchi?"

"Evidently that was her maiden name, and when *Signora* Nardo hired her sister-in-law to be the chef at the cooking school, they thought it would look more professional if she had a different name."

"That sure fits in with what the younger Moretti told me about her. He was not very impressed with her credentials. In fact, he made it quite clear she doesn't even have any credentials, and that the only reason she was hired was because her husband was blackmailing *Signora* Nardo about her affair with Giovanni. Evidently he threatened to tell her husband."

"That's becoming more than a coincidence, and you know how I feel about coincidences. What I don't understand is, if it's true, why Giovanni would be having an affair with her," Mike said.

"Well, let me answer that question with a quote from Shakespeare in Hamlet, 'There are more things in heaven and earth, Horatio, than are dreamt of in your philosophy.' In other words, we sure don't know everything."

"If we're going to solve this murder, we better find out everything."

"You're absolutely right. Mike, I've got to go back to the kitchen. It's my night for serving, and I sure don't want to make the chef mad, even if she isn't quite who or what she says she is."

"Try not to spill anything, and I'm looking forward to the risotto. It's one of my favorites, and I don't think you've ever made it for me."

"I always thought it would be too difficult to make, but now I feel pretty good about making it. The problem is it takes a lot of time to prepare, so it probably won't go on the menu at the coffee shop. See you at dinner."

CHAPTER FIFTEEN

"Kelly, I think today is even more beautiful than yesterday," Mike said as he looked out the window. "I loved the risotto last night. That's a definite make it at home dish, and I was particularly impressed you didn't spill the soup while you were serving it. By the way, I've never had chestnut soup before. It was delicious and went perfectly with the risotto."

"It was very good, but that gelato made the dinner for me. It's in my recipe packet, and I can't wait to try that one when we get home. Mike, I know I'm changing the subject, but do you hear something?"

"I sure do. It sounds like scratching at our door. Hold on; let me see what it is. Stay where you are. I'll take care of it." He walked over to the door and opened it. As soon as it was open, one hundred fifty pounds of fur bounded across the room, jumped on the bed, and began licking Kelly.

"Good grief, Kelly! Are you going to let Caesar stay there?" Mike asked as he laughed at the sight of Kelly pinned to the bed with a huge dog licking her face and wagging his tail.

"I don't think I have a choice in the matter. Looks like Caesar has become my new best friend. Lie down, boy, lie down." With that command, the massive dog stretched his full length out on the bed next to Kelly, and looked over at her with adoring eyes.

"I'll say one thing for him. He's well-trained. If I'm going to have to watch another male get in bed with you, I'm glad that at least it's only a dog," Mike said chuckling.

"What time is Chief Varano picking you up today?"

"Ten this morning, so I won't be here for lunch. Let's get dressed and go down to breakfast. I desperately need some coffee."

"Okay. Caesar, stay," Kelly said getting out of bed and walking into the bathroom. "Mike, give me ten minutes, and I'll be ready."

Mike sighed. He knew ten minutes to Kelly meant at least twenty-five minutes. He was right. Twenty-five minutes later Caesar, Kelly, and Mike walked down to the dining room where the continental breakfast was being served. When they'd finished eating, Kelly looked at her watch and said, "I think I'll go into the kitchen now. It doesn't make much sense for me to go up to the room and immediately turn around and have to come back down for class. Good luck today. Hope you and the chief make a lot of progress."

"I know he'd like to. See you, later. Enjoy the olive oil trip."

Kelly spent the rest of the morning helping to prepare the lunch and evening meals. Lunch was a simple meal of spinach and ricotta dumplings with a bean puree served on crostini and a green salad. Dinner was to be more elaborate, consisting of roasted lamb, green beans, a grilled pepper salad, and ending with something called "Granny's Tart." Kelly's only regret was that she couldn't be at all of the stations to see how each dish was prepared. She was resolved to the fact she'd have to use the recipes when she got home rather than relying on her experience of actually preparing the dishes

"As I mentioned the first night, we will take a field trip to a nearby farm with an olive grove and a small boutique olive oil processing plant following lunch," Chef Bianchi announced at the beginning of lunch. "If you want to go, please meet me at the hotel entrance at 2:00. We'll return to the castle around 4:00. If you've never seen how olive oil is made, I think you'll find it interesting."

At 2:00 Kelly joined a small group of students at the hotel entrance. Several of the students had preferred to spend the warm afternoon by the swimming pool. Kelly patted Caesar's head and told him she'd be back in two hours as she got into the van. She sensed a hint of sadness in his eyes as she boarded.

*****

A short time later Alberto drove the van up a lane lined with olive trees on each side as far as the eye could see. At the end of the lane were two buildings. The one on the left was clearly the commercial building where the olive oil was pressed. It was painted white and in big red letters were the words, "Rizzo Olive Oil." The one on the right was a large stone house with purple blooming wisteria covering its sides. Heavy wooden garage doors were on the left side of the front of the house. Next to the garage, curving steps led up to the wooden front door. On the left side of each of the steps brightly colored blooming flowers trailed over and down large terra cotta vases.

That's one of the warmest, most welcoming homes I've ever seen, Kelly thought. *If Giovanni was having an affair with Signora Nardo, I can't believe Signora Rizzo knew about it. The house speaks of happiness.*

The van pulled up in front of the commercial building, and the students got out and entered the building. The manager of the olive oil company met them at the door. "*Buongiorno* or good afternoon," he said. Welcome to Rizzo Olive Oil. Today I will be showing you the steps we take in making olive oil. Naturally, we have a much larger plant in Florence where we make the majority of the olive oil we sell; however, you will have a chance to see the process here. We begin with cleaning the olives. All rocks and sand must be removed, or they will damage a hammer mill like ours and will also quickly wear out the oil separator.

"Next, we will watch the olives as they are ground into a paste which helps release the oil from them. Then we mix the paste until small oil droplets combine into bigger ones. Although there are other steps that are optional such as additional processing or putting in additives, the last step is where the oil is separated from the vegetable water and solids. I'm sure you've all heard the term 'first press.' If we were still using presses, this would be the first press, but now it's done with the help of a centrifuge which separates the oil, water, and the solids separately. After the oil has been separated, it's put into tanks or barrels. At this facility we use barrels, but in Florence we use large stainless steel tanks. An additional step is sometimes done where we filter the oil. Those are the basic steps you'll be seeing during our tour. If you have any questions, please don't hesitate to ask me as we walk through the plant."

Although Kelly found the tour fascinating, she was more interested in what the mindset was of a woman whose husband had supposedly been the lover of a woman who had just been murdered. She wondered if *Signora* Rizzo knew about the rumors. When the tour had ended and the manager had escorted the students into the gift shop, so they could buy olive oil souvenirs and have some wine and crackers, she slipped out a side door. Kelly had no idea what she was looking for, but something told her to stay in the shadows of the olive trees, and see if she could find out anything.

She walked towards the rear of the house and stopped a moment to look at the view in front of her. Olive trees covered the landscape for as far as she could see. It presented a classic snapshot of the beauty of the Tuscany area. Looking at the back of the house she saw a large patio that was set back from the house with steps from the house leading down to it. The terra cotta vases she'd noticed on the front steps of the house were repeated with vibrant flowers and color everywhere she looked. She moved closer to the house, and when she was standing at the foot of the steps she heard a woman's voice coming through a nearby window and from the pauses it sounded as if she was talking on the phone. Kelly strained to hear what she was saying.

"Piero, she was murdered yesterday. Does this mean I need to send funds to your Cayman account? As I recall that was the agreement we had." She was quiet for a few moments and then asked, "What do you mean you'll let me know? Either you were responsible for it or not." She was clearly listening to the voice on the other end of the phone. "All right. I'll wait for your call. Since you don't know, I'm assuming you weren't personally responsible for doing it, but that someone you hired may have murdered her, and if so, you want me to deposit the money. Is that correct?" She listened some more to whoever was on the other end of the line and then ended the conversation with, "I don't know whether to thank you or not, but if it was you or someone you hired, thank you."

My instincts sure were right about this. It sounds like Signora Rizzo, if that's who was talking, hired someone to murder Signora Nardo. Obviously, she must have known about the affair. Now if I can just get back to the gift shop without being seen. Heart beating rapidly, she hurried back to the gift shop, walked in, and almost bumped into Chef Bianchi.

"I've been looking for you," Chef Bianchi said, "where have you been? It's almost time for *Signora* Rizzo to come here. She likes to personally welcome the guests to her property."

"I'm sorry, I had to use the restroom, and I noticed when we got out of the van that there was a separate building behind the main one with restrooms. I should have told you I was going there."

"It's not a problem." She turned away from Kelly and greeted the beautiful blond statuesque woman who was entering the gift shop. "Angelica, thank you so much for taking the time to come here today. My students have thoroughly enjoyed the tour, and I think many of them are taking your olive oil home as a souvenir. Would you like to say a few words?"

"Certainly," the voice Kelly had heard only a few minutes earlier say. "I want to thank you for coming, and I hope you enjoyed the tour. Now you know what goes into the process of making the olive oil we use so much of here in Italy and which is now very popular all over the world. I would stay longer, but I am expecting a very important phone call. Again, thank you for coming." She turned and hurried out of the building.

There is no doubt after hearing her speak that it was Signora Rizzo who was trying to find out if the person she'd hired to kill Signora Nardo was the one who had actually murdered her. Wow! That means she may have been responsible for the murder, but it certainly sounds like she didn't get her hands dirty doing it. Wait until Mike hears about this.

CHAPTER SIXTEEN

Kelly looked out the window of the van as it drove up the lane towards the castle, and she could make out Caesar's form on the bottom step, waiting for her. As soon as she got out of the van he walked over to her side and stood next to her.

"Hi, boy," she said. "Have a good afternoon? It's almost time for dinner. I'll feed you in just a few minutes." She stooped down and petted him. When she stood up, she realized the rest of the students and Alberto had all gone inside the castle. Something had been bothering her ever since she and Mike had arrived at the castle. She had no idea where the Nardos lived. The rooms on the second floor all seemed to be for the guests, and the only rooms she'd seen on the ground floor were the dining room, the kitchen, the library, and the large entryway which served as the hotel reservations area for the converted castle.

She looked around and still not seeing anyone said, "Caesar, take me to *Signora* Nardo's room. Can you do that? *Signora* Nardo's room. Go, boy, go."

The big dog pushed against her legs and started walking towards the side of the castle. He looked back at her as if to say, "Hurry up, Kelly. How are you going to explain this if anyone sees you?"

Caesar stopped at the side of the building in front of a large wooden door. She tried the doorknob, but the door was locked. Caesar pawed at the doormat and looked up at her. She bent down, put her hand under the mat and felt the cold steel of a key. She took a Kleenex from her purse and picked up the key, being careful to keep her fingerprints off of it. Kelly quickly looked around one more time, making sure no one was watching her. She put the key in the lock and opened the door, hoping no one was waiting for her on the other side. She gingerly walked in and saw several doors leading off of the hall. She said a silent prayer to whoever had the foresight to put the words *Signor* Nardo on one door and *Signora* Nardo on another. She listened for a moment in front of *Signora* Nardo's door and heard nothing. Kelly opened the door and quickly walked in, Caesar following her.

The large bedroom made her feel like she'd stepped into another century. While the parts of the castle she'd been in had been refurbished in bright colors with welcoming prints and plaids along with the antiques, nothing had been done to this room for what seemed like centuries. Everything in the room was red or gold. Kelly vaguely remembered reading something about red being the color of nobility during the Renaissance. With the exception of a modern king size bed, it didn't look like anything had been put in the room for hundreds of years.

This is unbelievable. I'm getting a serious case of claustrophobia, and I don't even know why I'm here and what, if anything, I'm looking for.

On the far side of the room she saw a door and opened it, remembering that the *Signor's* suite had been on the other side of the hall. This was clearly the *Signora's* office. It, too, was done in shades of red, but someone had decorated it with a much lighter touch. Instead of the heavy velvet drapes that were in the bedroom, pale red linen drapes were backed with sheer white ones to keep the sun from damaging them. Against one wall was a large Mediterranean pine desk. Kelly walked over to it. She wondered if the police had searched the room, because it didn't look like anything had been touched. *Signora's* calendar was on the desk as well as several invitations to local events.

I wonder where she kept the business files for the castle. There's no file cabinet. Maybe she used one of these drawers.

Kelly tried to pull a large side drawer open, but it was locked, as were the rest of the drawers.

Well, so much for that. I have no idea where to look for a key. She probably had it on a chain or something, and I don't have time to search for it.

"Caesar, we need to go," she whispered. "I can't find the key, and I don't want to get caught. Mike would be furious with me if he knew I was doing this."

She was petting him as she turned to go when her finger touched something on the underside of his collar. "Caesar, what's this?"

The big dog wagged his tail, and she would have sworn he smiled at her. She pulled his collar around and over, discovering that that what she'd felt was a key that slipped into a key slide. She reached in her purse for another Kleenex and easily pulled it out. She inserted it in the desk drawer and it opened easily. Kelly looked at Caesar and gave him a kiss on his massive head. "Thanks. Let's see what I can find."

As quickly as she could she looked at the files that were labeled in the drawer, glad once again that she'd retained the Italian she'd studied so long ago. Two of them caught her attention. One was a file marked "Wills" and the other was a file marked "Giovanni Rizzo." Although Kelly really wanted to spend some time seeing what was in them, she knew she was pressing her luck by staying in the room any longer. Without thinking of the possible consequences of her action, she shoved both the "Wills" file and "Giovanni" file into her large purse.

Kelly locked the drawer, put the key back in Caesar's key slide, and walked through the office door to the bedroom. She listened for a moment but couldn't hear anything. She quietly opened the bedroom door and walked down the hall towards the door that led outside. She looked around and still seeing no one, reached in her purse for the key to the outside door, locked it, and put the key back under the mat, making sure that the Kleenex she'd used to keep her fingerprints off of it when she'd gotten it out from under the mat was still wrapped around it.

She walked around to the front of the castle and she and Caesar walked through the front door and into the reception area. "Matteo, I think I'll feed Caesar this afternoon. I believe you said his food was kept in the dog run. How much should I feed him, and is someone else feeding Bruno?"

"I'm taking care of Bruno. Caesar gets about three cups of dry dog food and a can of dog food. The measuring cup is in the bag. Thanks for feeding him."

"No problem. I'll do it in a few minutes. I want to go up to my room and see if my husband's returned."

"I haven't seen him, but I haven't been at the front desk the whole afternoon, so he could have come back."

"Thanks," Kelly said as she and Caesar walked up the stairs. She felt like the purloined files were burning a hole in her large purse. She hoped against hope that Mike hadn't come back yet. She knew he would definitely not approve of her methods for getting information.

CHAPTER SEVENTEEN

Kelly put her key in the lock for the door of their room, hoping against hope that Mike would still be at the station with Chief Varano. When she was inside the room, she looked around, but didn't see him.

Thank heavens he's not back yet from his meeting with the chief. Now I can take a look at these files.

She sat down on the bed, reached into her purse, and pulled the files out. Caesar lay down on the bed beside her and was snoring within moments. She went through the papers that were in the Wills file and saw that *Signora* Nardo had clearly designated *Signor* Nardo as the sole beneficiary of her estate which made sense considering they had no children and that her parents had considered their son, her brother, to be incapable of managing the castle. She spent a few moments looking at the contents of the Giovanni Rizzo file and then gasped in surprise. Kelly was so absorbed in what she was reading she didn't hear the key being inserted in the door lock for their room. Caesar sat up suddenly and growled. He stopped when Mike walked into the room.

"So how was the olive oil excursion? Are you an expert in making olive oil now?"

"It was very interesting," she said, trying to shove the file folders back in her purse before Mike saw them.

"Kelly, I've been around you long enough to know that look you have on your face. What's going on?" he said, sitting down beside her on the bed and reaching across her to get the files. He took them out of her hands and looked at her quizzically. "Wills and Giovanni Rizzo," he said reading the labels on the tabs. "Kelly, where did you get these?"

"Mike, you know there's a complementary bottle of wine on the desk. Maybe you should open it and have a glass before I tell you about it."

"That's not necessary," he said in his serious sheriff's voice. "I want you to tell me how you got these files."

"Look, I know you're not going to be thrilled with how I got them, and that's okay with me. I just opened them, and I think you're going to be very pleased at what's in them and probably happy I got them for you."

"Ah, so now it's you got them for me. Kelly, let me repeat the question. How did you get these files?"

She told him how she and Caesar had managed to get into *Signora* Nardo's room and how she had found the key to the desk on the underside of Caesar's collar. "Mike, I think the important thing is what's in the Giovanni file." She took it out of his hands and removed some papers from it. "Look at this. It's a document deeding the legal title of *Castello di Nardo* to Giovanni Rizzo. It's not dated, and it's not signed. What do you make of that?"

"I'd say it just might be the smoking gun investigators always look for in a murder case. No, I am not in the least bit happy you took a risk like that. If someone had seen you, you could have been arrested for breaking and entering. I suppose the only thing that was in your favor was that *Signor* Nardo is grieving and still not seeing people, so he wasn't up and about when you entered their residence illegally. We tried all day to get him to see us, and he refused. That's probably why you were able to get those files. Her room hasn't been searched yet. I just hope to heck you were smart enough not to leave any fingerprints, because the chief is planning on having it dusted tomorrow, with or without the *Signor's* consent."

"Of course I was. Believe it or not, I've learned a lot from you, like not to leave my fingerprints on anything. I used a Kleenex for the keys and on the doorknobs I touched. So what do you think of this document?"

"Kelly, I'm going to have to show it to the police chief. All afternoon we've been searching for reasons why Giovanni Rizzo, a known skirt chaser of beautiful women, would be having an affair with *Signora* Nardo. It seemed completely out of character and didn't make any sense. The chief has talked to enough people that the rumors about the two of them having an affair seem to be true. It appears that they were indeed having an affair, and had been having one for quite some time. The chief has a number of contacts in Florence who were able to identify both of them from photographs he faxed them, and they confirmed that the two of them often spent the day at various hotels in Florence."

"Mike, I'm not a lawyer, but as I understand this document, if *Signora* Nardo signed it, she would be deeding the castle over to Giovanni, and her husband would not inherit it. Is my thinking correct?"

"Yes. That must be the reason for the affair. She was probably flattered by his attention, and he was using that as leverage to get her to sign the deed. What's troubling me is that it's certainly a motive for murder, but only if it was signed by her, and it doesn't appear that she ever signed it unless he has an original signed deed and this one was only for her records. That we don't know."

"If he has it, and if he records it with the local recorder's office or whatever they call it here in Italy, that would certainly be a motive for killing her."

"I agree, Kelly, it's a motive, but there would have to be solid evidence that he was the one, in fact, who murdered her."

"Yes, I see what you're saying. By recording the deed, his reputation would be in shreds. Not only would it appear to be a really sleazy thing to do, but his wife would be certain he'd been having an affair with *Signora* Nardo. By the way, I need to tell you what I overheard today. Mike, don't raise your eyebrows like that. I hate it when you do that. I just happened to overhear something I think you'll find interesting."

"You just happened to overhear something. Uh-huh. This better be good. Go ahead, I'm all ears."

She told him about the olive oil excursion and overhearing *Signora* Rizzo's conversation with someone. "Mike, what I'm wondering is this. If she hired someone to kill *Signora* Nardo, can she be charged with murder?"

"I imagine she could be charged with conspiracy to commit murder, but I'd have to check into the Italian law on it. The interesting thing is now we have two people who not only have motives, but *Signora* Rizzo, from what you heard, was actively trying to have *Signora* Nardo murdered."

"Mike, don't forget about *Signor* Nardo. If she signed the deed, and if he found out about it, he might have been angry enough to kill her."

"It means he doesn't get the castle, that's true, but at the moment, Giovanni has the most to gain. What I haven't told you is there are rumors that some of his clients have filed complaints with the Italian Bar Association. From what the chief found out today from the one located in Milan, apparently there have been three complaints filed against Giovanni for embezzling client's funds. All three are under investigation. The chief said he was told Giovanni had not been very cooperative in the investigation."

"If he's embezzling his clients' money, that's pretty serious. Isn't that a crime?"

"I'm sure it is, but it has to be proven and that can be very difficult to do. What usually happens is a lawyer says it was a bookkeeping mistake and replaces the money in whatever account he's being accused of embezzling. It's not all that uncommon. The chief is hoping to get more information on Giovanni's financial situation. He'd heard rumors that the olive oil business was not as financially successful as Giovanni has told people. There was also talk he was looking for investors who might want to buy it. All this makes me wonder about the man."

"I agree. So we have both of the Rizzos and *Signor* Nardo as possible suspects. A couple more who might also qualify are Berto Moretti, the owner of the other cooking school, and the *Signora's* brother. What I don't understand is why her brother would do something now. If he thought there was some way he could get the property, you'd think he would have done something long ago. Plus, from reading the *Signora's* Will, it seems pretty clear that the *Signor* was the sole and only beneficiary and there's wasn't any mention in her Will about her brother. The same thing is also true about *Signor* Moretti. Why commit the murder now and not at some earlier time?"

"I have no idea. I need to find out if the title to the castle was vested solely in her name. I'll make a note to ask the chief about that tomorrow. He's picking me up at ten again, so I'm going to have to bail on you. Some honeymoon. Me trying to solve a murder, you taking some cooking classes, and a one hundred fifty pound male dog instead of me in my wife's bed. This is not exactly what I'd planned."

"Mike, I'm still loving it. I've always wanted to go to Italy, and it's everything I thought it would be. Don't forget when we leave here we're going to Florence for a couple of days. I can't wait to see the Uffizi Museum and the Leonardo da Vinci Museum, plus I'm going to insist you buy me something gold on the *Ponte Vecchio*, you know, the bridge that spans the Arno River and has all the jewelry shops. I'm really excited about that. Tomorrow's the last day of classes, and even though the cooking school was only for three days, I feel like I've learned a lot, and I'm definitely going to put some of the recipes I've learned on the menu at Kelly's. We're taking a field trip tomorrow to the *Mercato Centrale* in Florence and I'm really looking forward to that. I've heard it's one of the most interesting markets in the world."

"I think I would have enjoyed that, and I'm sorry I have to miss it. Kelly, seriously, what are you going to do about Caesar? Shouldn't he be in his dog run or something and not in our bedroom?"

"I've been so busy talking to you I almost forgot I told Matteo I'd feed him. I'll be back in a few minutes."

"Okay. I want to see if there's anything in these files we've overlooked. I know the chief will be happy with the information you got, but very unhappy that you took the risks you did."

"Couldn't you just tell him the files showed up in our room and leave it at that?"

"No, Kelly, I won't lie for you."

"Okay, but we both know what a help I am."

"Don't push it, Kelly. Smart money knows when to keep their mouth shut and at the moment, you're not acting like smart money."

"Got it Sheriff. Back in a few. Come on Caesar, time for dinner."

CHAPTER EIGHTEEN

"Kelly, that was a fabulous meal. The lamb was perfect, and everything else was too. I have to tell you that Granny's Tart was one of the best things I've ever eaten. It wasn't too sweet, and it left a wonderful taste in my mouth. I'll be the first one down to breakfast tomorrow because Chef Bianchi said that the leftover tart was even better the second day, and I intend to have at least one more piece of it. Of course that's not including the pieces I'm going to have as soon as we're back home and you make it."

"Look around, Mike. You're not the only one who's going to be down here early. There's not a crumb left on any of the dessert plates. Almonds, pine nuts, ricotta cheese – what's not to like? It's definitely going on the menu at Kelly's Koffee Shop when we get home."

They were walking down the hall on their way back to their room when Mike's cell phone rang. He looked at the screen on his phone and said, "It's Chief Varano." He gave the room key to Kelly, so she could open the door while he talked to the chief.

"Chief, I'm just walking into my room. Let me close the door. I don't know what you're going to tell me, but it's been my experience whenever the chief of police calls it's probably not a call other people should overhear."

"Good thinking, Mike," the chief said. "We got a break in the Nardo murder case. You and I tried every which way today to figure out a way to look at Giovanni Rizzo's financial records, and we couldn't come up with anything. After I dropped you off at the castle and went back to the station, ironically enough there were two messages for me from clients of Giovanni. These were from two of the three people who had filed complaints against him with the Bar Association. What they told me was almost identical."

"Carlo, tell me one thing. Did they give you something we can use?"

"Without a question. Both of them said large sums of money had been drawn out of the trust accounts that were in their names as well as Giovanni's name. Neither of them had authorized the withdrawals. Both of them had immediately contacted him and questioned the withdrawals. He told them it had been an inadvertent withdrawal, and that he had simply made a mistake and taken the funds from the wrong account. He said it should have come from the account of one of his other clients."

"Seems like I've heard that before," Mike said. "I've known a few attorneys in the United States who have used the same excuse when they've been caught with their hand in the cookie jar, or as you'd probably say, taking money out of one of their client's accounts."

"The timing couldn't have been better. I have a very good friend who's a judge and happened to be the one on-call tonight if any search warrants needed to be issued. I called him and told him what had happened with the two clients, and that tomorrow I would like to search Giovanni's law office as well as the office in his home, if he has one."

"Were you able to get a search warrant?"

"Yes, it went into effect a few minutes ago. I had to go to the judge's home to get his signature, and I had to get signed statements from the two people who had filed complaints with the Bar Association and called my office. I intend to search Giovanni's office at 8:00 tomorrow morning. I'd like you to come with me. Two heads are better than one when it comes to something like this, and when we were talking earlier today you mentioned you had conducted a number of searches when warrants had been issued. You're probably far more qualified to carry this out than my deputies, although I will bring one of them with us."

"I'd be happy to accompany you, but I also need to tell you what Kelly found out today. I didn't want to bother you and figured I'd just tell you when I saw you tomorrow; however, this seems like as good a time as any." He told Chief Varano what Kelly had overheard at the Rizzo home and what she'd discovered in the files she'd taken from *Signora* Nardo's bedroom.

"You know I could arrest her for breaking and entering, plus stealing. That was not only a dangerous thing for her to do; she also committed an illegal act. I won't arrest her for it, but she needs to know I could."

Mike ran his fingers through his graying hair in frustration. "Carlo, you're not telling me anything I don't know, but if you knew Kelly, you'd know you wouldn't get anywhere by trying to tell her not to do something like what she did today. She justifies doing such things by saying she's helping me solve cases. Believe me, it drives me nuts."

"I can only well imagine. If my wife did something like that, I'd be furious. I think here in Italy we have a little more control over our wives than you Americans do."

"You're probably right, but it's also what makes her interesting. I really never know what she's going to do."

"Well, maybe it would be a good thing if you got her to promise to stay out of the case from now on. With the information both of us now have, we may be getting close to solving the murder. Anyway, I certainly hope so."

"So do I, Carlo. I'll talk to her. So, you'll pick me up around 7:45 in the morning?"

"Yes, see you then. Enjoy the rest of your evening."

Mike ended the call and turned to Kelly. "Did you happen to overhear what Chief Varano said?"

Kelly had suddenly become very busy examining her wedding ring and answered in a tiny voice, "Of course I heard him. Sounds like he's a male chauvinist."

"I don't know. I've never discussed that subject with him, but at least give lip service to me by promising you won't do anything more on this case. Can you promise me that?"

"Of course, sweetheart," she said, mentally crossing her fingers behind her back. "You have everything you need to solve it. I'll bet it's Giovanni, and I wouldn't want to do anything that might jeopardize your position with the chief, but you have to admit, the information I gave you was pretty good."

"Once again, you got lucky, Kelly. It was nothing more than being in the right place at the right time."

"Sheriff, as I recall, you're the one who doesn't believe in coincidences. Do you think that hearing about *Signora* Rizzo and finding those files are coincidental? Just answer that," she said defiantly.

"Kelly, this conversation is officially over. I am not going to argue with you while we are on our honeymoon in Italy about whether or not your actions today were deliberate or coincidental. Instead, I'd like to invite you to step out on the terrace with me and look at that full moon shining on the vineyards and the olive grove. It's really beautiful."

"It may be beautiful, but does that mean neither one of us will get much sleep tonight? I know I sure don't sleep very well when there's a full moon."

"With Caesar staying in our room, I don't think there will be any other reason we won't get much sleep tonight. Once again, so much for the romantic honeymoon I'd looked forward to."

"Mike, when we get to Florence, we'll have our honeymoon. I'll have my new gold bracelet that you're going to buy me from one of the shops on the *Ponte Vecchio*, and I'll thank you properly for it then. Caesar will have to stay here. From the looks the staff gives him every time they see him, he'll have a good home. Oh, one other thing. Does this mean you won't be talking to *Signor* Nardo tomorrow?"

"I have no idea. It probably will depend on what we find out when we search Giovanni's office. Why?"

"No reason. Just curious."

"Kelly," Mike started to say, but she leaned over and kissed him.

"Mike, we've talked enough, and we're both tired. Tomorrow looks like it's going to be just as busy as today. We need to get some sleep."

"All right, but don't forget. I want to get up early, so I can have some leftover Granny's Tart with my cup of coffee in the morning."

"No problem. You know how prompt I am. I'm sure we'll be the first ones to get down there."

He raised an eyebrow and looked at her. "Sweetheart, I know how good your intentions are, but if for some strange reason I happen to get ready before you do, I'll meet you in the dining room."

"Okay. Love you. See you in the morning."

He glared at Caesar who had opened one large eye as if he were winking at Mike. Mike turned off the lamp on the nightstand. His last thought before falling asleep was how romantic it was with a one hundred fifty pound dog at the foot of the bed. He was sure if he touched Kelly, Caesar would attack him and take his leg off. He hated to admit it, but the dog thoroughly intimidated him.

CHAPTER NINETEEN

When Kelly stepped out of the bathroom the next morning, she realized Mike had already left for breakfast, so he wouldn't miss out on getting a piece of Granny's Tart. She just hoped he'd saved her one.

She walked downstairs and took Caesar out to his dog run before she went into the dining room. "Aah, Kelly, there you are. I saved you a piece of Granny's Tart, but when you hadn't come down for twenty minutes, I thought maybe you were going to skip breakfast this morning, so I ate it." He smiled and tried to look sorry. He wasn't able to pull it off.

"Mike," she said, "let's be honest. How long was it before you ate the second piece, my piece, of Granny's Tart?"

"I'm going to be just as truthful with you as you oftentimes are with me. I waited twenty minutes."

"I seriously doubt that," she said taking a sip of the coffee she'd gotten from the serving table when she walked into the room. "Mike, I've really gotten to like Italian coffee. It's more like an espresso. We might have to get one of those machines when we get back home."

"Okay, your call. I see the chief standing in the reception area. See you whenever. Love you."

"Be safe, Mike. You may be helping to solve the murder, but promise me you won't try to be a hero."

"I promise, but then again if my promises are as good as yours, not sure what it's worth. See you later," he said grinning. He stood up and gave her a half-salute.

Kelly walked over to the table where the continental breakfast was laid out. It was hard to decide what to choose with such an array of mouth-watering dishes in front of her. There was a platter with skewers of sweet Italian sausage and peppers, biscotti, croissants, miniature pizzas with bacon and scrambled eggs kept warm in a chafing dish, and a big bowl of fresh fruit with a pitcher of cream. The only thing that kept Kelly from trying one of everything was the knowledge that lunch and dinner would be equally wonderful, and she knew if she ate a large breakfast she wouldn't be able to do justice to the other two meals. After a lot of mental debating she ended up with a biscotti and a small dish of fresh fruit, so she could enjoy what she'd be making in class that morning.

When she was finished eating, she walked outside and let Caesar out of the dog run. "Come on, boy. I've got a little time before class, and I need to email Julia."

Her daughter Julia and her husband Brad, along with his young daughters, had just moved into Mike's deceased aunt's home in Calico Gold, California. When Mike married Kelly he'd become an instant stepfather to her two adult children, Julia and Cash. With the marriage of Brad and Julia, Mike's family had once again increased, as he became a step-grandparent to Brad's two daughters who were now four and six. Never having had children, he loved every minute of family life, but it certainly was a change from his life as a divorced man of many years.

I can't believe this ancient castle has Wi-Fi. It's almost sacrilegious, but I'm glad I don't have to go to the village to email Julia, Kelly thought.

She spent the next half hour telling her daughter about Italy, the castle, and the cooking school. She deliberately left out the part about

Signora Nardo being murdered, knowing how worried Julia got about Mike's cases and her involvement in them. She looked at her watch. "Caesar, it's time to go to cooking school. You can stay outside the kitchen while I'm in there. Let's go."

"Aah Kelly, there you are," Chef Bianchi said. "Today I would like you to prepare the stuffed focaccia with grilled zucchini, peppers, pesto, and mozzarella. You've made the focaccia before, so go ahead and make it according to the directions. When you finish making it, you will put the stuffing ingredients on it. It's kind of like a pizza, but there's one thing to remember, never put the mozzarella on the bottom. It gets really soggy if that's done."

"I thought we were going to change partners every day, but for the last two days I've worked with you, and quite frankly, you've been busy with the other students. I'm worried I'll make a mistake. I think I've been lucky so far."

"The reason I haven't gotten another partner for you is that you're very good in the kitchen. You have great instincts, and you really are a seasoned cook. Trust me, you can easily do this. We'll have it for lunch. When you finish the focaccia, you can prepare the braised artichokes with potatoes, parsley, and garlic we'll be serving for dinner. It's served cold, and it's even better when it's made a few hours ahead of time. Do you have any questions?"

"Not now, but I probably will once I get into the recipes."

Chef Bianchi patted Kelly's arm and said, "You'll do just fine. I have no doubt. Oh, by the way, how are your husband and the chief doing with solving *Signora* Nardo's murder?"

"There was a breakthrough last night. I think they're getting very close to solving it."

"Who do they think committed such a horrible crime?" the chef asked.

"The one thing I've learned as a sheriff's wife is that it's not my case. It's my husband's, and believe me he tells me often that it's not my case. You better ask him."

"Do you think he'll be back in time for dinner?"

"I really don't know. He enjoys law enforcement work, but he's loved the food here and has really been sorry that he couldn't attend class. Between you and me, I think what he's sorriest about is that he isn't here to enjoy the fabulous meals."

Two hours later, tired and hoping she hadn't disappointed the chef, Kelly joined the other students as they made their way to the porch for the luncheon they had just prepared. Kelly looked at the table and wished she'd brought her phone with her so she could take a picture of it and send it to Julia. The luncheon meal was served family style with large bowls and platters of the food they'd prepared set on the long table. Today they were having spinach gnocchi, the stuffed focaccia Kelly had made, a fennel salad with lemon and mint, and for dessert, panne cotta, which was a light pudding-like dish sweetened with vanilla. The colors and textures made her mouth water.

The wine steward told them about the wines he'd selected for the meal, and soon everyone was happily eating and drinking. Kelly had noticed during the morning class that Chef Bianchi seemed very nervous, and when she looked across the table at the chef, she noticed what appeared to be lines of tension around her eyes and mouth.

I wonder what she's worried about. Well, you never know what's going on in someone's personal life. I really don't know anything about her other than she's married to Signora Nardo's brother, and I'm not supposed to even know that.

When everyone had finished eating lunch, Chef Bianchi stood up and tapped her knife against her water glass. "Students, I want to remind you that this afternoon we will take an excursion to the *Mercato Centrale* in Florence. It's well worth seeing, and I hope all of you will join me. Since it is a one hour trip each way, our last dinner of the cooking school will be later than usual. Wine will be served at

7:30 in the library and dinner will be 8:30. Those of you who are going on the excursion meet me at one-thirty in the hotel entrance, and we will board the van."

This is one thing I definitely want to do, Kelly thought as she walked to the hotel entrance with Caesar by her side. "Caesar, you stay here and I'll be back in a couple of hours." She got on the van with the other students, looking forward to visiting the world famous *Mercato Centrale* in Florence.

CHAPTER TWENTY

Kelly thoroughly enjoyed the drive into Florence. It was like a step back in time. The driver told the students he was taking the old road into Florence since it was more scenic and provided many interesting things to see. He said they'd come back on the newer highway, but he thought they'd enjoy the quaint views the old road provided. He was absolutely right. They passed through numerous little villages with old churches and stone castles visible in the distance and miles of vineyards and olive groves. At one point the van stopped to let a shepherd and his sheep cross the road. Kelly watched the sheepdog herd his charges as they crossed the road. The dog looked in both directions first, and only when he was sure no cars were coming would he allow them to cross the road.

Everywhere they looked another jewel was unearthed such as villages with walls that had been there for centuries. Sunflower fields in full golden bloom were next to green vineyards and olive groves. Beech and chestnut trees dotted the landscape. Kelly understood why chestnut soup had been served the other night. Evidently the nut was very abundant in the area, and the chef had mentioned that Italians like to use what they grow. In the distance she saw medieval towers that looked like sentinels protecting what was in the realm below them.

Dramatic, she thought. *There is no other word that can do justice to what I'm seeing. It is just unbelievably dramatic.*

The closer they got to Florence the heavier the traffic became, and once they were in Florence it was like being in every other large city in the world. Too many cars trying to fit into streets that had never been designed for them.

Chef Bianchi began to speak, "In a few moments we will be at the market, but before we get there I want to point out a couple of things of interest to you. In the distance you can see the red tiled dome of the *Duomo* or the Cathedral de Santa Maria dei Fiori. I'm sure you've all heard about it but in case you haven't, it took one hundred seventy years to build, and it is famous for its pink and green marble. I know some of you are going to spend time in Florence when you leave the *Castello di Nardo,* and I hope you'll spend some time at the *Duomo.* There is nothing else like it anywhere in the world.

"The second thing I want to point out is the *Ponte Vecchio.* You can see this ancient bridge in the distance where it spans the Arno River. It withstood the German invasion in World War II and also the overflowing flood waters of the Arno River on several occasions. Until 1218 it was the only bridge that crossed the Arno. There had always been shops on the bridge, such as butchers and others, but in 1593 Ferdinand I decreed that from then on only goldsmiths and jewelers would be allowed to have shops there. He said it would help the people. I think the only thing it helps now," she said laughing, "are the shopkeepers who cater to the tourists. The bridge is known all over the world for its gold and jewelry shops, and I venture to say that most of the tourists who come here buy something from the shops."

Well I'm going to be one of them, Kelly thought, *and I don't care how schmaltzy it is. I'm going to remember how beautiful this area is and how wonderful the food was every time I wear whatever it is Mike's going to buy me.*

Chef Bianchi resumed speaking, "The building we are now approaching is the *Mercato Centrale.* If we become separated, we will meet at four-thirty next to the bronze boar statue you can see next to the entrance. No matter what your food preferences may be, you will find them here. I hope you brought a camera, because this market really is amazing. I believe this is a place for people to explore on their own, so while I will be with you, I won't be conducting a tour as such, but feel free to ask me any questions you might have. I'll be happy to interpret for you if you wish to speak to a shopkeeper. Oh, one other thing. The shopkeepers will call out to you with their specials of the day, and if you want to buy something, keep in mind that haggling is considered an art here. It is rare to ever pay the asking price of anything here at the market. Have fun."

Kelly had never been comfortable traveling in groups, so while the rest of the students slowly moved as a group from stall to stall, she walked up the stairs to the second floor and began exploring the vast array of food that seemed to stretch endlessly. Chef Bianchi was absolutely right. No matter what kind of food you wanted, the *Mercato* had it, and probably in all the varieties in which it could be made. For the next two hours, she explored shops that ranged from ones that specialized in salty Tuscan prosciutto to shops that specialized in sheep's milk cheeses. There were pastas of every kind, dried and fresh, as well as more loaves of every kind of bread than she had ever seen in her life displayed on simple wooden shelves and in barrels. She was glad she'd visited the second floor first because most of the stalls that sold food to go were there. Since she was still relatively full from lunch, even though everything tempted her, she didn't buy anything to eat.

Quite some time later Kelly looked at her watch and realized she only had a few more minutes before she was to meet up with the group. She wandered into a produce section on the first floor, and seeing some produce she had never seen before, asked the woman working in the stall what kinds of vegetables she was selling. She asked the question in English as most of the shopkeepers spoke English well enough to converse with the tourists, but this woman replied, "I no speak English."

Kelly switched to Italian and learned that the woman was filling in for her sister who had become ill that morning. She told Kelly about the various different vegetables that were on display and how to cook them. They talked to each other for several minutes. As Kelly turned to leave she saw Chef Bianchi walking out of an adjacent stall and hurrying towards the entrance. She looked back at Kelly with a perplexed look on her face.

That's strange. It's almost as if she didn't want me to see her. Wonder what that's all about. Oh well, time to go.

CHAPTER TWENTY-ONE

The students arrived back at the castle about six o'clock, and just as he had done the day before, Caesar was waiting for Kelly by the front door to the castle. As soon as she stepped out of the van, he loped over to her, covering her with wet kisses. "I'm glad to see you, too, big guy."

She bent down and petted him while the other students and the chef went into the castle. Kelly stood up, intending to follow them, but something stopped her. She faintly heard what sounded like angry voices coming from the direction where the Nardos resided in the castle. Kelly looked around and didn't see anyone. Nonchalantly she strolled over to where three olive trees stood next to the window of the *Signor's* living quarters and stepped behind them. "Caesar, come," she whispered. The big dog followed her. She gave him a hand movement, and he sat down.

The voices she'd heard were male voices, and she could just make out what they were saying.

"Now that my sister is dead, this castle is rightfully mine, and I'm going to file a lawsuit to get it and have you thrown off the property."

That must be Salvadore Nardo, the chef's husband, Kelly thought.

A second man Kelly was pretty sure was *Signor* Nardo responded. "What are you talking about? As her husband, Tonia willed the property to me. We both made Wills several years ago that designated the other one as the sole beneficiary of our property. I intend to file the papers tomorrow. Tonia didn't believe in maudlin funerals, so I had her remains cremated. Now I can get on with what must be done. The police chief wants to talk to me, but I know nothing about her death. What I do know is that the *Castello di Nardo* is mine, and I want you to get off of my land. I don't know what ever made you think you had any right to the land in the first place."

"It is the land of my ancestors. The Nardos have owned this land for centuries. My mother told me when she and my father were making out their Wills and giving the land to Tonia that they had put a clause in the Wills stipulating if anything ever happened to her, the property would go to the closest person who was a Nardo. That would be me. There is no one else who should inherit that property. The castle is mine."

"You fool," Stefano laughed mockingly. "Your mother told you that just to keep you from making a huge scene when Tonia inherited it. I know they gave you a great deal of money to make up for it. Tonia told me you lost it all because of gambling. There is not and never was a document stipulating that you or any other Nardo should have the castle and the land. Tonia named me as her sole beneficiary. I looked at the Will last night, and it said something to the effect that no one other than Stefano Drago, who has taken the Nardo name, shall inherit any part of the *Castello di Nardo*."

"So who did she hire to draw up the Will? Was it Giovanni Rizzo?"

"Why do you ask?" Signor Nardo said in a steely voice.

"If he drew it up, you can plan on it that he doctored the Will so it wouldn't show that I should have the property if anything happened to Tonia."

"Why would he do that?"

"Everyone knows that he and Tonia were having an affair. If you didn't know about it, you're the fool, not me."

"Let me tell you a couple of things. First of all Tonia hired a lawyer in Florence to draw up our Wills. Secondly, whether or not she was having an affair with Giovanni Rizzo makes no difference to me. Our marriage had become nothing more than a marriage of convenience. If she was having an affair with Giovanni, so be it. I have had my share of affairs. She's dead now, and it really doesn't matter, but I'm not dead, and I am the one she named as her heir. I've had enough. Get out of my house and off of my property, or I will call the police chief and have you arrested. There will be no reading of the Will, since I am the only heir. Let me write down the name and phone number of her attorney, and you can confirm it with him. I'll call him and tell him I told you to call and ask if you are named in the Will as a beneficiary. Once the Will is filed with the court it will be public knowledge. Here's his name and phone number."

"You do that, but let me tell you one thing. Your loving wife was having an affair with Giovanni Rizzo. Everybody knew about it and referred to you as a cuckold. Yes, you're the one who's the fool. Why do you think Tonia hired Luisa to be the chef at her cooking school? We both know she's a good cook but hardly the best in Italy. I told Tonia if she didn't hire Luisa, I would tell you about the affair. That's why Tonia agreed to hire Luisa. It had nothing to do with Lucia's cooking skills, although she does seem to be doing a good job as the chef at the school."

With those words, Salvadore grabbed the piece of paper out of Stefano's hand and stomped out of his living quarters. It happened so quickly that there was nothing Kelly could do but hope he was angry enough he'd go directly to his car and not see her hiding behind the trees. She was in luck. A few minutes later she heard a car driving rapidly down the lane to the highway. She stayed there for several minutes trying to digest what she'd just heard.

I've got to tell Mike about this. Evidently the Signora's brother thought he was going to inherit the property if Tonia died. If he thought that, it makes him a suspect, because he would have a very good reason to murder her. Mike always says to figure out who has the most to gain from the murder. It looks like a lot of people thought they would gain something if she died. Signor Nardo says he's the one who will inherit the property. If Signora Nardo did deed the property over to Giovanni Rizzo prior to her death, he would wind up owning the property. I can't forget about Signora Rizzo. She wouldn't get the property, but she'd probably get her husband back if Tonia was dead. And last but not least, there's Berto Moretti. He wouldn't be getting the property either, but he'd be getting rid of his competition. Why can't Mike ever get a case where there's just one suspect?

She looked around and didn't see anyone. "Caesar, let's go." The big dog had been sitting next to her and waiting for direction from her. At her words he stood up and followed her into the castle and up to her room.

CHAPTER TWENTY-TWO

He's got to be wrong, Salvadore thought, as he drove as fast as he could back to the small village. I know mother wouldn't lie to me. The castle rightfully belongs to me. Lucia and I will be living there soon. Stefano is trying to get me to give up my rightful claim to the Castello di Nardo. I'm the one who is a true Nardo, not him. That wimp even took the name of Nardo to please Tonia. I'll call the lawyer as soon as I get back to the house, and I know he'll tell me that I'm the one who will inherit the castle. I'm surprised he hasn't already called. Yes, Stefano is just trying to scare me, so I won't make a claim on the property. I'll have good news for Luisa when I talk to her tonight. She told me to call her after my meeting with Stefano.

He parked his old car next to the weed infested yard in front of their house, and walked up the broken sidewalk to the front door. *Sure will be glad to get out of this dump. It's a far cry from a castle, that's for sure.* Salvadore walked quickly to the kitchen and opened the freezer, taking out an icy bottle of grappa. He uncapped it and drank it straight. *That's how the peasants do it. Guess I'm a peasant now, but that will all change when I have peasants working for me in the castle. I'll be drinking aged grappa out of a special cognac glass. No more unaged grappa for me.* He wiped his mouth with the back of his hand and poured some grappa into a dirty glass.

The warmth of the grappa relaxed him, and he took the piece of paper with the name of the lawyer from the pocket of his simple grey shirt. The shirt and the black pants he wore were the best clothes he had, and he'd wanted to look like he belonged in the castle when he'd visited his brother-in-law.

Salvadore sat down at the small kitchen table in the room which also served as their dining room and living room. Besides the front door that led into the room there were two other doors. One door led to their bedroom, and the other door led to a small bathroom which had a leaky shower and a toilet that seemingly never stopped running. Every time Salvadore used it, he thought about how it needed to be fixed. He'd usually feel bad after going in there and needed a small little glass of grappa so he'd feel better. He knew a lot of things needed to be done to the little house, but there was never any extra money to do them, and like he'd told Luisa, he couldn't work because of his back.

He picked up the phone and held it to his ear as his shaky hand dialed the number on the paper. In a moment a young woman answered the phone. "This is the law office of *Signor* Conti. How may I direct your call?"

"I would like to speak with *Signor* Conti. Is he available?"

"*Sì*. May I tell him who is calling?"

"Tell him it's *Signor* Nardo, Tonia Nardo's brother."

"He'll be with you in a moment, *Signor.*"

Salvadore picked up the glass of grappa and drained it as he waited for *Signor* Conti to come on the line. In a few moments, a voice said, "*Signor* Nardo, this is *Signor Conti*. How may I help you?"

"My sister, Tonia Nardo, died a few days ago. I was told by our mother that if anything ever happened to Tonia, the castle was to revert to her nearest Nardo relative, which would be me. I understand you wrote her Will."

Signor Conti hesitated a moment. "Normally, I would not reveal the contents of a Will until it has been filed with the Court, but with her death there is no longer an attorney-client relationship. Her husband, *Signor* Nardo, or as he is also known, Stefano Drago, inherits the *Castello di Nardo* and everything in it. She named him as her sole beneficiary."

"No, that can't be," Salvadore said in an agitated voice. "My mother told me a clause had been put in my father's and her Wills that stipulated if anything happened to Tonia the castle would revert to me. It simply can't be."

Signor Conti took a deep breath and began to speak. "I'm sorry, *Signor* Nardo, but there was no such stipulation in your parents' Wills. I drew them up, and I also drew up Tonia's Will. Your parents' Wills were filed with the court when they died in the automobile accident, and I processed the estate which they willed to Tonia. Tonia left everything to her husband. I'm sorry you were given this misinformation, but I remember your mother telling me something about it. I believe she told me, and forgive me, that you had a gambling problem, and she didn't want the castle to be sold because of your debts. She told me that she had told you it would revert to you, but she also told me that she said that only to placate you. As I recall, you inherited quite a large sum of money when your parents died. Your parents felt that if you gave up gambling and were gainfully employed, Tonia would do something to help you, and she was told that by them. Since Tonia never mentioned she was helping you, I can only assume your situation hasn't changed."

"So what you're telling me is that I get nothing, and that silly fool my sister married gets everything. Is that right?"

"If you prefer to look at it that way, you are correct. Again, I'm sorry that you've thought you would inherit something all these years. I'm going to have to end this conversation, because I'm due in court in a few minutes. Thank you for calling and good luck to you." With that, he ended the call.

Salvadore sat with the phone in his hand, stunned. *Stefano was right. I get nothing.* He hung up the phone and walked over to the freezer. He took out the grappa bottle and poured himself another glass.

What now? What will Luisa think? I promised her when we were married that someday we would live in the castle. It's probably the only reason she married a loser like me. I know Stefano won't keep her on as the cooking school's chef. He'll probably hire that chef Luisa overheard Tonia talking to, Elena Oberti. What will we do for money? I can't work, and the only other place that has a cooking school is the Moretti Palazzo, and I know he'll never hire her.

He took a long drink from the glass trying to figure out what to do next. *Maybe Luisa can find work in one of the little cafes in the village that cater to tourists.* He took another drink and looked at his watch. *She told me to call her after I talked to Stefano to see when we would be moving into the castle. I better not call her now. She's probably doing the last of the preparations for dinner. I'll wait until after dinner and call her then. What if she leaves me? I've wondered if the only reason she stays with me is because of the castle.*

He looked around the pathetic little room and for the first time realized there was a definite possibility that very soon he might be out on the street with nowhere to go. Luisa had inherited the little house from her parents, and it was hers. The more he thought about it, the more he was certain she would leave him. For the first time in his life, he had no idea what he should do, and he knew with a sickening certainty that Luisa didn't really care about him. He had no one.

CHAPTER TWENTY-THREE

Kelly opened the door to their room, hoping that Mike had returned from spending the day with Chief Varano. She quickly looked around, realized he wasn't there, and from the looks of the room, she was pretty sure he hadn't been back. She took her cell phone out of her purse and called him.

"Hello, sweetheart. How's your day been?" Mike said when he answered the phone.

"Interesting, but I want to hear how the search went. Did you find out whether or not Giovanni was embezzling funds from his clients?"

"Yes. We found some files that clearly indicated he was embezzling funds. The stupid man left a paper trail that was really easy to follow. He'd written down the dates he'd taken funds from each account. It was pretty easy to go to his personal account and see where he had deposited the exact same amount into that account. We also brought in a computer expert to find out if he there's anything on the computer we should know about or that's incriminating. He's got the computer and said it would take a couple of days."

"How did *Signor* Rizzo take it?"

"As expected. Not well. We found out something else that is quite interesting. Evidently he has a mistress, and he's paying for an apartment for her in Florence. When we found the credit card receipts for it in a file, Carlo sent the information to a friend of his who's on the Florence Police Department. Within an hour he got back to Carlo with the woman's name and a photograph of her. She's a real beauty."

"Wow! That man's been busy. Gives a new meaning to being a Romeo. He's got a wife, according to everyone he was having an affair with Tonia, and now he also has a mistress. Did you find out anything about Tonia deeding the castle over to him?"

"No. We found a file with her name on it, but the only thing we found in it was the same deed you found yesterday, the one that had never been signed by her. After seeing the photograph of his mistress and talking to his wife today, which I'll tell you about in a minute, I have to believe that the only reason he was having the affair with Tonia was to get her to deed the castle over to him. She sure wasn't the beauty that the other two are. It looks like the castle will go to *Signor* Nardo with no strings attached."

"What happens to Giovanni now?"

"Carlo arrested him for embezzlement. He'll be arraigned tomorrow and will probably plead not guilty. If he can post bail more than likely he'll be released afterwards. Carlo told me it would be very rare in an embezzlement case for the person not to get out on bail. What was interesting was when we went to his house."

"I want to hear all about it, but isn't that home and the land it's on beautiful?"

"Yes. It was exactly like you'd described it. We didn't call first as we preferred to surprise *Signora* Rizzo. You never know what a spouse will do in a situation like this. Sometimes they'll try to leave town or cover up evidence if they think they can be implicated. She didn't do either one of those things, but I'm not sure I've ever seen anyone that angry. I think she was sincere about not knowing anything regarding the embezzlement.

"Carlo asked her if she knew about the apartment in Florence. He wanted to see what her response would be. From the way she acted, I'm sure she didn't know anything about it. When he told her about it being rented to a young woman, she was furious. Between her husband being arrested for embezzlement, finding out he had a mistress in Florence, and having someone, she didn't tell us who, confirm that her husband was having an affair with *Signora* Nardo, she was in a rage. She screamed she wouldn't give him one penny from her trust fund to help him out, and even though she'd never believed in divorce before, she did now. And the tirade went on and on. I can't begin to tell you the awful things she called Giovanni."

"Did you discover anything at the house?"

"Not really. He had an office there, but about the only things in it were bills and receipts relating to the olive oil business and the house."

"Do you really think *Signora* Rizzo will divorce him?"

"If today was any indication, I don't think there's a shadow of doubt that if she hasn't called her attorney today, she will tomorrow to start the proceedings. She said it was a good thing she had a large trust fund she'd inherited from her parents, because it looked like her husband had been lying to her for years about his assets."

"So even though you found out about the mistress and the embezzling, there was nothing to indicate he murdered *Signora* Nardo."

"No, not a thing. We know nothing more about that than we did when we started looking into it two days ago. I know we're leaving for Florence tomorrow, but if it's all right with you, I thought we could go in the afternoon. Instead of traveling with the rest of the students in the van to Florence, Carlo told me there's a train that leaves from the village for Florence. He even said he'd drive us to the train station. That way I could be with Carlo when he talks to *Signor* Nardo. You don't mind, do you?"

"Not at all. I wouldn't mind spending a little more time with Caesar. Anyway, I've had a very interesting afternoon. Can you talk a few more minutes, or will you be back here in time for dinner? If you're going to be, I'll wait until then to tell you."

"No. Carlo just ordered some pizza for us. He'll take me back to the castle in a couple of hours. Go ahead without me."

"Will do, but I do have a couple of things you'll probably want to tell him."

"Shoot."

"Well, you know I went to the *Mercato Centrale* today. Oh, by the way, while I was talking to one of the shopkeepers, I would swear that Chef Bianchi was eavesdropping on my conversation. When I turned away from the shopkeeper I saw her, and she hurried away. Several times on the way back I caught her staring at me. I can't figure that out."

"Kelly, while that's interesting I don't think it's something Chief Varano is going to be particularly interested in."

"That's not what I was going to originally tell you. I just thought of it, and I'm curious about it. Anyway, I overheard a huge argument between *Signor* Nardo and his brother-in-law, the chef's husband. Here's what happened."

She spent the next few minutes relating how she happened to hear the conversation, where she was standing when she heard it, and what the two men had said during the exchange.

"So what do you think, Mike?"

"I think we should start living in Italy, so you'll keep your promises to me like the chief says the Italian women do. Maybe I need to be a little more chauvinistic."

"That's not funny. I just happened to overhear something when I was standing near some trees."

"Oh, Kelly, Kelly, Kelly. Whatever am I going to do with you? It makes me sick to think what might have happened to you if Salvadore had spotted you as angry as you say he was. The last thing he'd want is a witness to his conversation with *Signor* Nardo. I love you Kelly, and at times I don't think you have a clue how much danger you're in. This was one of those times. I'll be glad when we can leave the castle and all of the suspects behind us. Maybe I'll be able to keep you safe then."

"Look at it this way, Mike. All that's left is the last dinner tonight, and then I'll come back to the room and go to bed. Tomorrow I'll spend a little time with Caesar, and we're off to Florence. What can possibly happen in that short period of time?"

"I don't know Kelly, but if anything can happen to you, I'm sure it will. I'll see you in a couple of hours."

Mike was absolutely right. If anything could happen to Kelly, it would.

CHAPTER TWENTY-FOUR

Kelly walked out to the dog run and fed Caesar. Then she went into the library and joined the other students for their last evening at the castle. She had mixed feelings about leaving tomorrow and continuing on to Florence. She'd thoroughly enjoyed the cooking school and what she'd learned from it. She felt far more confident about preparing Italian food than she had in the past, but she didn't like to leave something undone, and the *Signora's* murder was still unresolved.

"I'd like a glass of white wine. Whatever you recommend is fine with me," she said to the wine steward. "What do you do when the cooking school isn't operating?" she asked.

He looked around to see if anyone was listening and then said, "Don't tell anyone, but I'm the wine steward at the Moretti Palazzo when they're conducting a cooking school. It's been very fortunate for me that the cooking schools are never held at the same time. At the Moretti Palazzo there is also a restaurant, and when I'm not being the wine steward at either one of the schools, I'm the sommelier at Moretti's Ristorante. I'm really very fortunate that I can do what I love in a village this small."

"Tell me something. I met Berto Moretti's son when I visited their shop, *Cucina*, the other day, and he seemed very nice. I've heard conflicting things about the two cooking schools. What's your opinion about them?"

Again he looked around to make sure no one was listening to their conversation and said, "Berto's son is a wonderful young man. He's nothing like his father. Berto has a very bad temper which I don't think his son inherited, or if he did, he's learned to control it. I've never seen him angry. Even if I wasn't working here at the school when it's in session, I would know when the *Castello di Nardo* is getting ready to have another cooking school. Berto becomes impossible to be around. He has never forgiven *Signora* Nardo for making the castle into a hotel with a cooking school. He is very jealous of the success of the castle and quite frankly, there are times when the Moretti cooking school is not full. He and his son like to tell everyone that their cooking school is much better than the one here, but that is not true. Many times he has talked about how much he hates her."

"Why do you think that is?" Kelly asked.

"*Signora* Nardo was not the easiest person to be around and certainly not the warmest, but she paid her staff well. I've never heard a complaint from anyone who has stayed at the hotel or has attended the cooking school. She was always able to get better help than *Signor* Moretti, and I think that's the difference. The grounds here are spotless. The ones at the Moretti Palazzo, not so much. It's like that with everything. It's kind of like the old saying; you get what you pay for. He wasn't willing to pay for the best, and it's reflected at the Palazzo. The kitchen here is state of the art. *Signora* Nardo spared no expense when she had it installed. The Moretti kitchen is dingy and doesn't have any of the high technology things one finds here."

"May I ask you something personal?" Kelly said.

"Sure, I don't mind."

"Are you paid more here than at the Moretti Palazzo?"

He grinned. "Oh, yes, far more. Plus the wines I serve are a much better quality than what he buys. It's the little things, but even if the students and guests aren't consciously aware, somehow I think they know."

"And the reason you continue to work for *Signor* Moretti is so that you can do what you love in this small village, is that correct?"

"Yes. My family has been here for centuries, and there is nowhere else I would rather live. Of course I could make more money if I worked in Florence or Rome, but my wife and I have two small children, and we want to raise them here, where we both grew up."

"I don't want to keep you from the other guests, but thank you so much for taking the time to tell me all of this."

She looked at her watch and saw that it was almost time for dinner, and she didn't want to be late for the last dinner, particularly since the main course was a beef filet served on a bed of lettuce with a truffle salad. She'd always heard about Florence beef, and tonight she was going to have her first taste of it. Who knew? If she really liked it, she'd have it again when she and Mike were in Florence.

Kelly put her wine glass down and joined the other students as they made their way to the dining room. *This was incredible* she thought, as the meal drew to an end two hours later. *What a dinner. I'm so sorry Mike missed it. He would have loved it. What's not to love about the beef, the gratin of tomato with anchovies which Mike loves, the braised artichokes with potatoes, parsley and garlic, topped off with the limoncello dessert, which was fabulous? I can make that at the coffee shop. What could be easier than vanilla ice cream and lemon sorbet with a couple of splashes of limoncello liqueur on it? Yum, yum.*

After she finished dinner, Kelly left the dining room and went to the dog run to get Caesar. Little did she know that in the very near future the big dog would be the reason her life would be spared.

CHAPTER TWENTY-FIVE

"There you are," Kelly said to the big dog as he stood up and walked to the front of his dog run. "Time to go up and see how Mike's day was. Caesar, come." The two of them walked into the castle and started up the stairs.

"Darn," she said when they were halfway up the stairs. "I left my apron in the kitchen, and I don't want the cleaning crew to throw it out. I want to take it home as a souvenir. I'm sure they'll be doing a thorough cleaning job since the cooking class has ended. Come on, Caesar, I need to go back to the kitchen. Mike will just have to wait a few minutes." She turned around, walked down the stairs, and headed towards the back of the castle where the kitchen was located.

On her way to the kitchen she passed by the library and saw Domenico, the wine steward. She walked in and said, "Need some help? Caesar and I are on our way to the kitchen. We were halfway up the stairs when I realized I'd left my apron in the kitchen, and I was afraid the cleaning crew would throw it out. I didn't want that to happen. The apron, along with some cookbooks I bought at *Cucina*, are my only souvenirs from the cooking school. We paid plenty to attend the cooking school, and since Mike has barely even eaten a meal here, I have to say they've done well by us."

"No, but thanks. Every night I take the wine out of the library and decide if there's enough left in the bottles to return any of them to the wine cellar which is next to the kitchen. If there are only a few drops left in a bottle, I throw it out, which is usually the case, but tonight there are two bottles that are almost full."

"Since the class has ended and there won't be a lot of people around, who gets the leftovers?"

"It seems like there are always people willing to drink what's left of the wine. Some of the staff has a glass of wine after they finish work, and the *Signor* and *Signora* always enjoyed their wine. People know it's here. I won't serve a wine that's been opened for more than three days." He put a trash barrel containing the empty bottles in the hall. "The cleaning crew takes care of the empty bottles for me, and they also take the glasses to the kitchen where they'll be put in the dishwasher. All I have to worry about is doing something with the leftover wine."

She looked down at Caesar. "You'll have to stay in the hall. You know the rule about no dogs in the kitchen." She turned to Dominico. "Where is the wine cellar? I don't think I've seen it."

"It's not really a cellar. We just call it that. It's on the other side of the kitchen. When the *Signora* renovated the kitchen, she had it installed. It's temperature controlled, soundproof, and there's room for 1,500 bottles. I have to walk through the kitchen to get to it. I'll put these two bottles in the wine cellar, and then I'll go home. It's probably too late to see my children tonight, but at least I'll have a chance to see my wife for a little while. If you don't mind, I'd like to ask you something."

"Certainly. What is it?"

"You said 'we were halfway up the stairs.' Does that mean you let Caesar stay in your room at night?"

"Yes, why do you ask?"

"I'm just thinking he must love it. He was very much the *Signora's* dog, but she never allowed him to sleep in her room. Maybe it's an

Italian thing, but I don't know of anyone who lets their dog sleep in the same room where they do."

"Could be. Both of our dogs at home sleep in the bedroom with us. It must be cultural thing. I never thought about it."

"I'm sure Caesar's happy with the arrangement."

The three of them walked down the hall towards the kitchen. Kelly opened the kitchen door for him and at the same time motioned for Caesar to stay where he was. She looked back at him as she and Dominico walked into the dimly lit kitchen. They heard a voice at the far end of the kitchen and saw someone who looked like Chef Bianchi talking into a cell phone with her back to them. From the tone of her voice, they could tell she was very angry. Dominico laid the bottles down on the counter and the two of them stood silently side by side as they listened to Chef Bianchi speak into the phone.

"What do you mean you won't be inheriting the castle? You told me before we were married that if anything happened to your sister, you would be the one to inherit it." She listened a minute. "Of course *Signor* Nardo told you that. What did you expect, you stupid fool! Did you think he'd tell you the castle would be yours now that Tonia's dead, and he was happy to move out and give it to you?" Again she listened.

Kelly knew she should leave, but she was rooted to the spot on the floor where she was standing. Also, she wanted to hear what Chef Bianchi was saying, as she had a sense it could be very important in solving the murder.

"You called the lawyer who wrote up your parents' Wills and Tonia's Will, and he told you that you had no legal right to the castle property? Are you sure?" Her next words utterly shocked Kelly and Dominico. "The reason I killed Tonia was so we could finally be the owners of the castle. Do you know what will happen to me if anyone finds out? And I did it for you, you idiot. Don't start sniveling. I'll think of something. Maybe it's time to take care of the *Signor.* If he's not around, you would be the only one left, and then we could have the castle. Yes, that's what I'll do. You told me a long time ago to keep a gun with me for protection. Well, guess what? I just took it out of my purse, and it's time the *Signor* joined the *Signora*."

Just then one of the bottles of wine that Dominico had placed on the counter rolled off and shattered on the kitchen floor causing the chef to whirl around. They both saw the gun in her hand. "Don't move. Stay where you are or I'll shoot," she said to them in a menacing manner. She spoke into the phone, "Sal, I have some other work to do. I'll be home in a little while."

"You were the one who murdered the *Signora*?" Dominico asked incredulously. He couldn't believe what he'd just heard. "I've worked for you since the cooking school opened, and the *Signora* hired you as the chef. She was your sister-in-law. How could you do such a thing? I can't believe this."

"Well you better, because you two are next. I can't let you live knowing what you do now and Kelly, I know you speak Italian. I heard you at the *Mercato*."

In a shaky voice filled with fear, Kelly said, "All right, Chef Bianchi, I can understand that you murdered *Signora* Nardo because you thought your husband would inherit the property, but what I don't understand is why did you do it now and not years ago?" Kelly wished she hadn't left her purse with her cell phone back in the room. There was no way for her to get in touch with Mike. She didn't notice that Caesar was no longer sitting at the spot outside of the kitchen door where she'd left him.

"I did it because I overheard her talking to Elena Oberti, the chef who's on television, and the chef everyone is talking about these days. I knew she was going to let me go, and I couldn't have that. Anyway, the castle is rightfully my husband's and with Tonia alive, there was no way he was going to get it."

"What made you think your husband would get the castle rather than her husband?" Kelly asked.

"When Sal proposed to me he said his mother had told him there was a clause in her Will stating that in the event of Tonia's death, the castle would be bequeathed only to a Nardo, and my husband was the only other living Nardo. I knew someday it would be ours. I simply made it happen a little sooner rather than later," she said giggling. "Just like the two of you are going to die a little sooner than you thought you would. We've talked long enough. I want both of you to go into the wine cellar. The walls in it are very thick, and it's soundproof, so when I pull this trigger, no one in the castle will hear a thing."

"Since you're going to kill us anyway, would you tell me how you poisoned *Signora* Nardo? I've been trying to figure that out, and I can't."

"It was easy. I ground up sleeping pills and put them in special cookies which I gave to her maid. Everyone knew Tonia liked to have a little sweet before she went to bed. Her maid always came into the kitchen to get something to take up to her. I waited for an hour and went up to her room. She never locked her door. I went in and put a needle in her arm with the poison in it. It was so easy I should have done it a long time ago."

At that moment the loud blast of a gunshot reverberated through the kitchen. The gun which had been in the chef's hand flew to the floor and she clutched her bleeding hand and cried out in pain as she fell to the floor.

"Don't move," Mike yelled, walking over to the chef and kicking her gun away from where she'd dropped it. "Kelly, pick her gun up and keep it on her while I call Chief Varano."

CHAPTER TWENTY-SIX

"Carlo, it's Mike. You need to come to the castle immediately and bring a couple of men. Kelly's holding a gun on the person I'm pretty sure murdered *Signora* Nardo. It's Chef Bianchi. I don't know the details, but I'll find out and fill you in when you get here." He turned to Kelly. "I'll take the gun, but I have to ask, what were you two doing here in the kitchen?"

"We didn't know she'd be here or that she was the one who murdered *Signora* Nardo. I'd left my apron from the cooking class in the kitchen, and Dominico was getting ready to take a couple of bottles of wine back to the wine cellar when I saw him in the library. We walked here together, and when we got here we overheard her talking to her husband. Unfortunately, one of the bottles of wine rolled off the counter and shattered on the floor. When she heard the crash she turned and saw us. Honest. Now I have a question for you. How did you know I'd be here, and what made you come here with a gun?"

"Your friend here," he said, motioning to Caesar who was standing at the entrance to the kitchen. "I'd just opened the door to our room when he came racing up the stairs and literally head-butted me toward the stairs. He ran down them and then looked back to see if I was following him. I had my gun with me, and I figured when you weren't around, and Caesar was in that much of a hurry, something must be happening to you. I was right. I just followed him, and he stopped at the kitchen door. I stood there for just a few moments before I ran in, so you'll have to fill me in on everything she said. I don't speak Italian, but the gist I got was that she was going to kill both of you."

"Mike, she's the one who killed *Signora* Nardo." Kelly told him what she and Dominico had overheard and what *Signora* Bianchi had said to them about *Signor* Nardo being next."

"I thought it was her when I realized what was happening, but prior to that I never suspected her. It seems out of character, and she was the *Signora's* sister-in-law. You just never know about people. Even after all I've seen, I still get surprised," Mike said.

Dominico was pale and shaking when he turned to Mike and said, "May I leave? I really want to get home to my wife and children. I've never been involved in anything like this, and I feel sick."

"I'm sorry, but I know the chief's going to want to talk to you and have you tell him exactly what you saw and heard. I imagine your story and Kelly's will be identical, so it's pretty much a formality. Would you like to use my phone to call your wife?"

"Please."

Mike handed it to him, and Dominico walked to the far side of the kitchen to make his call. Kelly turned to Mike and said, "Where did you get the gun? I remember you decided not to go through the hassle of trying to bring one into the country, and you left yours at home."

"The chief gave it to me. Since the murder took place at the castle, and people knew I was involved in trying to solve it, he was worried that someone might try to do something to me. I never imagined you'd get in a situation where you'd need a gun."

"Believe me, neither did I. You know I almost feel sorry for her," she said, looking at Luisa softly sobbing on the floor. "She's lived most of the last twenty years or so believing that someday she would be the one to live in the castle and run it. Not only is that never going to happen, she'll probably go to prison for a long time for committing murder and attempting to commit more. The *Signor* has no idea how lucky he is that we wandered into the kitchen and Caesar found you, because if that hadn't happened she would have killed him."

"Actually, I'm the lucky one. If Caesar hadn't found me, more than likely you wouldn't be standing here right now."

They heard the sound of sirens getting louder and within minutes Chief Varano strode into the kitchen, followed by two of his policemen. "Mike, what's going on?"

Mike told him what had happened. The chief turned to his men. "I want you to handcuff *Signora* Bianchi and take her to the station. Book her for murder and attempted murder. When you finish, go to her home and tell her husband what's happened. Kelly, Dominico, I need to take statements from both of you. May I have your permission to record your statements? If you allow me to do that, it will save you a trip to the station to sign a written statement there."

Kelly and Dominico both told him that would be fine, and each of them gave him their version of what had happened from the time they had entered the kitchen. When they were finished, the chief turned to Mike and said, "I'm going to need a statement from you as well. How did you happen to show up at the perfect moment?"

Mike told him about Caesar, and how he had overheard enough standing outside the kitchen to cause him to come in and shoot the chef's gun out of her hand.

"What is going on?" they heard a voice ask, and a moment later *Signor* Nardo walked into the kitchen.

"I heard sirens and looked out my window to see the blue and red lights on two police cars. I saw one of them leave. What has happened? Why are all of you in my kitchen? Chief Varano, we've met before. I know you've been calling me wanting to talk to me about Tonia's murder, but I am so heartbroken, I couldn't do it."

The chief told him what had happened and that Chef Bianchi was the one who had murdered his wife. The man was clearly distraught about his wife's death and finding out that his sister-in-law had been the one who murdered her only added to his grief.

Kelly told him about the conversation they had overheard between the chef and her husband. She also went on to tell him she had overheard the argument between Salvadore and him earlier in the day.

"I told him the castle had been willed to me by Tonia, and that he had no right to it. He didn't want to believe that. From what you are telling me he must have called *Signor* Conti and found out from him that what he'd believed for over twenty years wasn't true. In a way I feel sorry for him. I wonder what will happen to him now that Luisa will be going to prison."

The police chief's phone rang and he listened for a few minutes. He pressed end and turned to face *Signor* Nardo. "*Signor*, I'm sorry to tell you this because I know you've had enough shocks the last few days to last a lifetime, but my deputy went to Salvadore's house to tell him about Luisa and discovered his body. He had committed suicide. It was very apparent from the position of the gun and his hand. Additionally, there was an empty bottle of grappa next to him."

Signor Nardo walked over to a chair and sat down heavily in it. Everyone was quiet, and then he spoke. "The family I have known for the last twenty years is gone, gone in a few days. Tonia murdered, Sal committing suicide, and Luisa going to prison, probably for life. I don't know how I can go on."

Dominico walked over to him and said, "*Signor* Nardo, your staff loves you. We want you to continue to use the castle as a hotel. See if the chef your wife was talking to will take over as the chef of the cooking school. You have several rooms that are not being used here at the castle. Why don't you make those into a restaurant? I will be your sommelier, and we will create a restaurant worthy of Michelin stars. I'm sure that would appeal to the new chef as well. Have her create signature dishes. Yes, you can never go back to the life you had, but that doesn't mean you can't have a new and wonderful life. Many of us would like to help you. Please, let us."

Signor Nardo looked up and said, "Thank you. I appreciate that. Maybe getting completely involved in something new would help me get over these losses. Come back tomorrow, and let's talk about this. Do you really think we could have a Michelin star restaurant here at the castle?"

"No, I don't think so, I know so. It would be an honor to help you." He held out his hand, and the *Signor* shook it. Dominico looked at the chief and said, "May I leave now?"

"Yes, and thank you."

"I did nothing. I think the hero tonight was Caesar. By the way, I have two little boys who would love to have a big dog. If no one has spoken for him, I would love to have him."

"Consider it a gift from the *Castello di Nardo* for your life being in danger. From what I learned tonight, I imagine *Signora* Reynolds would like one more night with him, but since I inherited everything that was Tonia's and that includes Caesar, it would be my pleasure for you to have him. When you come tomorrow you can take him with you."

Dominico walked out of the kitchen, petting Caesar on the head as he left.

"I think that's everything," Chief Varano said. "It's getting late, and it's been a long day for all of us. Mike, I'd still like to talk to you tomorrow and wrap up a couple of loose ends. Is it okay with you if I pick you up about ten?"

"Of course, Carlo. I'm happy to help in whatever way I can. With everything that's happened, I think I'll keep the gun with me tonight and return it to you tomorrow."

"Let's hope it won't be needed. Kelly, thank you very much for everything. I hate to say this, but without you I'm not sure this murder ever would have been solved. You American women are different from the Italian women. You don't listen to your husbands, but in this case I'm glad you didn't. Good night."

Kelly, Mike, and the *Signor* walked out of the kitchen and were joined by Caesar. "Would you like me to accompany you to your residence?" Mike asked *Signor* Nardo.

"No, thank you. I think it's very safe now. We have security here at the castle, but who would have thought we'd have to worry about one of our own?"

"Absolutely no one. Good night," Mike said. He, Kelly, and Caesar headed up the stairs, looking forward to a good night's sleep.

CHAPTER TWENTY-SEVEN

The next afternoon they took the train into Florence from the village and from there a taxi to the hotel where they would be staying for the next two days. The beautiful old brick hotel was very close to the massive cathedral and when they'd made the hotel reservations, they'd requested a room that overlooked the *Duomo*. The bellboy opened the room for them and put their luggage on the luggage racks. He pointed out some of the features of the room and asked them if they would like some ice.

"No, thanks," Mike said as he gave the bellboy a tip.

"Mike, did you do this?" Kelly asked.

"Did I do what?"

"Arrange for this his huge bouquet of flowers. It's absolutely gorgeous. I can't believe it. Thank you so much. That's the most romantic thing you've ever done," she said, walking over to him and hugging him while she kissed him.

"Darn. Hate to tell you this, but they're not from me."

"You're kidding! Who else knew we were going to stay here? I didn't even tell Julia or Cash we'd be staying here, and my staff has my cell phone in case there's a problem, so I didn't see any need to give them our itinerary."

"Is there a card with the bouquet?" he asked.

"I was so sure it was from you, I didn't even think to look." She walked over to the large bouquet. "Yup. I can see a little white envelope. I'll get it out. Who knows? Maybe I have a secret admirer."

"A secret admirer sending you flowers on our honeymoon? That wouldn't set real well with me. Open it up, and let's see what it says."

She tore the envelope open and read, "*Signora* Reynolds. I want to thank you once again for solving the murder of *Signora* Nardo. Enjoy the flowers while you are in Florence, and although I know Mike said he was going to buy you a keepsake at a jewelry shop on the *Ponte Vecchio*, please don't buy anything there. They are known to be tourist traps. Tomorrow afternoon there will be a package for you at the front desk of the hotel. Enjoy it and thank you again. It's signed by Chief Varano." She put the card down on the desk and turned to Mike.

"What a nice thing for him to do," she said. "Did you tell him I'd asked you to buy me something from one of the jewelry shops there?"

"I think I might have said something in passing. What do you make of his comment about a package for you being at the front desk tomorrow afternoon?"

"I have no idea. You're the one who spent all the time with him. He may be a male chauvinist, but he sure has good taste in flowers. I'll call him tomorrow and thank him. I am so excited to be here. Let's wander around for a couple of hours and then eat at a romantic little Italian ristorante that serves pasta. I'm starving for some. I thought I'd get a lot more of it at the cooking school, but we really didn't get much at all. Okay with you?"

"Absolutely. That sounds delicious. Tomorrow we can visit a couple of museums. I really want to see Michelangelo's David, and I definitely want to go to the Uffizi Gallery. Other than that, I'm pretty open. After the art we can go to the *Ponte Vecchi* shops. They may be tourist traps, but they're known worldwide, and we can at least say we've seen them. The chief told me there's a very good restaurant in the square beyond the *Ponte Vecchi*. We can have lunch there. Are you about ready to go?"

"Give me five minutes."

Swell. Might as well sit down and see if I have any messages on my phone. Knowing Kelly, it will be at least twenty minutes.

Thirty minutes later she said, "I'm ready. See, that wasn't so bad, was it? I'm really getting much better at being ready on time. You can stop the raised eyebrow routine. This is our honeymoon, if you remember."

"Oh, I remember. It was the murder and Caesar that got in the way of it. Maybe we can resume tonight when we get back."

"Just might do that, Sheriff. Now, let's get some pasta and get a sense of the lay of the land."

*****

"Mike, my brain can't take in any more art. Seeing the David was one of the high points of my life, and I loved the Uffizi, but let's go to the *Ponte Vecchio*. I really want to see it."

They got in one of the waiting cabs, and Mike told the driver to take them to the *Ponte Vecchio*. They wandered from one jewelry store to another, amazed at the array of gold and other jewelry that was on display.

"Mike, I know the chief said this was a tourist trap, but I'm really tempted to get something from here. I probably won't pass this way again."

"Let's hold off. He said there would be a package for you at the front desk this afternoon. Since he said it in conjunction with telling you not to buy anything here, let's see what's in it. If you still want something from here, we have plenty of time to get it tomorrow. Our plane doesn't leave until late afternoon. Deal?"

"Deal. Right now I'm ready to eat. All this walking is making me hungry. Did he tell you the name of the restaurant on the square?"

"No, he couldn't remember it, but he said I couldn't miss it because it had a bright red awning and the name was written on it in white letters."

"Mike, there it is," she said a few minutes later. "It looks like we were supposed to eat here. There's only one empty table." They hurriedly walked over to it and sat down.

"The chief was definitely right," Kelly said an hour later. "That was the best seafood pasta I've ever had, and the bread was just as good. How was your lasagna?"

"Every bit as good as your dish. All this walking, the food, and a glass of wine have made me sleepy. Can I interest you in going back to our room and taking a nap before we head out again?"

"That sounds wonderful. I wonder if the package has arrived yet."

When they got to the hotel, Kelly walked over to the clerk who was standing behind the front desk. "Excuse me, my name is Kelly Reynolds. I was told a package was going to be delivered to the front desk for me. Has it come yet?"

"*Si, Signora.* A man just brought it a little while ago. Here it is."

"Thank you." She and Mike walked over to the elevator. "Mike, it's really light. What do you think it is?"

"I have no idea. Honest. He didn't say anything to me about this or the flowers. You can open it as soon as you get to the room. Can you wait that long?" he asked in a teasing manner.

"Barely, just barely." Mike opened the door of their room, and she walked over to the table and chairs next to the window that overlooked the *Duomo*. Kelly took the small package out of her purse. It was wrapped in white tissue paper and tied with a red bow. She carefully took off the wrapping paper and the bow which covered the box. She removed the lid and took a note off the white cotton that covered whatever was in it.

"Well, read it. What does it say?" Mike asked. "I'm as curious as you are."

"Enjoy this small gold statue of Saint Lorenzo. He is the patron saint of cooks and also the patron saint of the cooking school that's located in the *Mercato*. I hope you will think of Italy with pleasure each time you look at him, and it's a small token of my appreciation for what you have done for me. This little statue was made for you by one of my relatives who is a jeweler."

She lifted off the cotton and gasped as she reached into the box and withdrew the two inch solid gold statue of Saint Lorenzo. It had a small bezel at the top, so it could be worn as a necklace or bracelet. She looked at Mike with tears in her eyes. "This is the most beautiful thing I've ever seen. Look at the workmanship. I don't know how anyone could make something this intricate and small out of solid gold. I'll treasure it."

"Here. Let me see it." He turned it over in his large hand. "Kelly, I don't know what this cost, but it couldn't have been cheap, and I don't think the chief is a wealthy man. I wonder how he could afford to give you this."

"I don't know when I've been so touched. This is far more beautiful than anything we saw in the *Ponte Vecchio* shops. And what a thoughtful gift. I take back everything I ever said about him being a male chauvinist."

"Well, where does that leave me? Am I off the hook for purchasing a piece of jewelry for you?"

"Mike, a woman can never have enough jewelry. Let your conscience be your guide."

"Kelly, are you the least bit familiar with the term enough is enough?" he asked, putting his arms around her.

"Nope, and I never want to be."

RECIPES

LIMONCELLO DESERT

Ingredients

1 pint lemon sorbet
1 pint vanilla ice cream
6 oz. limoncello or any Italian lemon liqueur
1 lemon, zested
Biscotti (any kind)

Directions

Place one scoop each of lemon sorbet and vanilla ice cream in a small bowl. Top with 1 ½ ounces of the lemon liqueur. Sprinkle the zest on top. Serve with biscotti.

PORK LOIN ROAST WITH MILK

Ingredients

2 lb. boneless pork loin
1/3 cup butter
2 medium sized fresh tomatoes, coarsely chopped
2 leeks, finely chopped, white and light green parts only

4 cloves of garlic, peeled and finely chopped
1 stick of celery, diced
4 tbsp. fresh thyme leaves
3 cups milk
1 tsp. salt
1 tsp. pepper
¼ cup flour
String

Directions

Preheat the oven to 400 degrees. Place an ovenproof pan with deep sides on the stove top and melt the butter over medium heat. Add the tomatoes, leeks, garlic, and celery and cook until soft. While the vegetables are cooking, put the thyme leaves on a cutting board and spread to about the width and length of the pork roast.

Roll the pork loin over the thyme and tie lengthwise with a long piece of string and then tie three times around the width. Pat with salt and pepper. Dust the pork with the flour, increase the heat to medium-high and brown, pushing the vegetables to the sides.

Heat the milk and pour it over the pork. Transfer the browned pork and vegetables to the oven and cook for 35 minutes. Remove the pan from the oven, put the pork on a serving platter and let it rest for 5 minutes. If the milk sauce is too thin, thicken with a mixture of water and flour and add to milk until desired consistency.

(I have found it makes a nice sauce thickening on its own.) Slice the pork into thick medallions, pour a small amount of the sauce over them and put the rest of the sauce in a serving bowl, letting people serve themselves.

TORTA DI NOCE (Calabrian Walnut Cake) with Strawberry Balsamic Sauce

Ingredients

12 oz. walnuts
4 eggs, separated
8 oz. sugar
1 lemon peel, finely grated
1 lb. fresh strawberries
4 tbsp. powdered sugar, divided equally
1 tbsp. balsamic vinegar
9 inch springform pan
3 tbsp. water

Directions

Preheat oven to 350 degrees. Grease and flour a 9" springform pan. Put walnuts in a blender or food processor and finely chop. With an electric mixer, beat the egg yolks and sugar together until pale and creamy.

Fold in the ground nuts and grated lemon. Beat the egg whites until stiff and carefully fold into the nut mixture. Gently pour into the prepared pan. Bake for 50 minutes until cake rises and is firm. Cool. When cool remove the cake from the pan and sprinkle with 2 tbsp. powdered sugar.

To make the strawberry sauce, hull and halve the strawberries and place in a saucepan with 3 tbsp. water and remaining 2 tbsp. powdered sugar. Heat slowly until soft and mushy. Pour into a food process or blender. Add balsamic vinegar and blend until smooth. Pour into a bowl, cover, and chill.

Serve the cake in thin wedges with the strawberry sauce drizzled over the top and down the sides.

BRAISED ARTICHOKES with Potatoes, Parsley & Garlic

Ingredients

6 medium sized artichokes
1 lemon, quartered
1 head fresh garlic
4 tbsp. extra virgin olive oil
1 small bunch of flat leaved parsley, roughly chopped
2 lbs. new potatoes, peeled, and cut into chunks
½ tsp. salt
4 cups water

Directions

Squeeze the lemon quarters into the water. Trim and then quarter the artichokes, putting them immediately in the lemon water. Peel off the first layer of skin from the head of the garlic and cut into six wedges.

Heat the oil in a large Dutch oven type pan. Add the garlic and parsley and sauté until the garlic is slightly colored. Add the artichokes, potatoes, salt and water. Bring to a boil, lower heat and simmer, uncovered, for about 20-25 minutes or until vegetables are soft and most of the water has evaporated. Can be served hot or cold.

CROSTATA DELLA NONNA (Granny's Tart)

Pastry Ingredients

7 ½ oz. slivered almonds
3 oz. sugar
14 oz. cake flour
Pinch of salt
Zest of 1 orange
10 ½ oz. unsalted butter, cubed in small pieces and chilled

3 eggs
Water

Note: All ingredients and utensils must be chilled several hours prior to preparation. Make the pastry a day before you wish to serve it.

Directions

When chilled, place in food processor and pulse to reduce almonds to a powder. Transfer to mixing bowl and gently mix with a hand mixer. Add flour, salt, zest, and mix. Add butter and mix until just incorporated.

Add eggs, one at a time and pulse on and off until large loose crumbs start to form. If too dry, add a few drops of water. Turn the bowl over and remove dough. Press dough into a ball and knead a couple of times. Don't over process.

Wrap ball in saran wrap and refrigerate for one day. There is enough dough to make two tarts. If you only want to make only one, freeze half the dough. Will keep for two months in the freezer.

FILLING INGREDIENTS:

3 oz. raisins soaked in a few tbsp. of warm red wine
2 cups plus 1 tbsp. milk
Peel from one lemon
4 eggs, separated
4 oz. sugar
4 tbsp. corn starch
10 ½ oz. ricotta cheese
3 ¾ oz. sugar for whipping egg whites
Large bowl of cold water

DIRECTIONS

Preheat oven to 350 degrees. In a large saucepan bring milk and lemon peel to a boil. In a separate bowl whisk egg yolks, sugar, and corn starch   until thoroughly mixed. Remove the lemon peel and pour hot milk on top of egg mixture, stir well. Pour the mixture back into the saucepan and place over medium heat.

Bring to a boil, stirring constantly until it forms a smooth cream. Transfer to a bowl set in ice cold water. Stir from time to time to prevent a skin from forming on the surface. It will develop into a custard-like filling. Sieve the ricotta cheese in a strainer to release the liquid and add it and the drained raisins to the cold custard.

Whip the egg whites with the remaining sugar until they form soft peaks. Fold them into the custard. Place the pastry in a Pyrex 9" dish so it covers the bottom and sides of the dish. Pour the mixture onto the rolled out pastry and level the top with a spatula. Put in the oven and check after 20 minutes. Filling should be just barely set. Let cool. Cut and serve. Enjoy!

ABOUT THE AUTHOR

Dianne lives in Huntington Beach, California with her husband Tom, a former California State Senator, and her boxer puppy, Kelly. Her passions are cooking and dogs, so whenever she has a little free time, you can find her in the kitchen or in the back yard throwing a ball for Kelly. She is a frequent contributor to the Huffington Post.

Her other award winning books include:

Cedar Bay Cozy Mystery Series
Kelly's Koffee Shop, Murder at Jade Cove, White Cloud Retreat, Marriage and Murder, Murder in the Pearl District, Murder in Calico Gold

Liz Lucas Cozy Mystery Series
Murder in Cottage #6, Murder & Brandy Boy, The Death Card

Coyote Series
Blue Coyote Motel, Coyote in Provence, Cornered Coyote

Website: www.dianneharman.com
Blog: www.dianneharman.com/blog
Email: dianne@dianneharman.com

Newsletter
If you would like to be notified of her latest releases please go to www.dianneharman.com and sign up for her newsletter.

Made in the USA
Monee, IL
19 March 2020